MURDER
AT
THE BIG T LODGE

A Liz Lucas Cozy Mystery - Book 6

BY

DIANNE HARMAN

D1607779

Published by: Dianne Harman
www.dianneharman.com

Interior, cover design and website by
Vivek Rajan
www.RewireYourDNA.com

ISBN: 978-1533669940

CONTENTS

Acknowledgments

ACKNOWLEDGMENTS

As always, thank you for spending your valuable time reading my books. I love writing them, but without loyal readers like you, I wouldn't be a successful author. This is book number 6 in the popular Liz Lucas Cozy Mystery Series. I hope you like it as much as you've enjoyed the books in my other three cozy mystery series, Cedar Bay, High Desert, and Midwest.

Here's a little backstory on how this book came to be written. I, like so many others, recently read about the death of Antonin Scalia, a United States Supreme Court Justice, who died unexpectedly while he was at a hunting lodge in Texas. What fascinated me was the Texas law stating that if there are no signs of foul play and a justice of the peace is not available, (often the case in counties with small populations), the death certificate can be signed by a judge without the judge having to make any kind of inquiry as to the cause of death or even seeing the body. I was amazed that such a law existed, and began to think about its ramifications. This novel is a book of fiction, so therefore it's a figment of my imagination, but that imagination was fueled by the circumstances surrounding the death of Justice Antonin Scalia.

I'm completely indebted to the two people who help make every book of mine a bestseller. First there is Vivek, who patiently formats my books for both print and digital, as well as designing wonderfully inventive book covers. I've come to rely on his ability to sense what the cover should be when I don't have a clue! The second person is my husband, Tom. He's very careful to make sure my books are as error free as possible, particularly as to time sequence and characters. Many times he's caught me having written the wrong name or the wrong place! Thanks to both of you!

And as I usually do, I need to thank my dog, Kelly, for finally leaving the puppy stage! I'd like to say she was the inspiration for my first cozy mystery, Kelly's Koffee Shop, but the truth is we got her after I'd written the book, thus she had to have the name Kelly!

Finally, you may wonder why the dog in this book is a bullmastiff. I can't answer that other than to say the breed fascinates me. We've owned boxers for years, and they kind of look like miniature bullmastiffs, so that might be the reason! Hope you enjoy the read!

Amazing Ebooks & Paperbacks for FREE

Go to www.dianneharman.com/freepaperback.html and get your FREE copies of Dianne's books and Dianne's favorite recipes immediately by signing up for her newsletter.

Once you've signed up for her newsletter you're eligible to win autographed paperbacks. One lucky winner is picked every week. Hurry before the offer ends.

CHAPTER ONE

"So, my love, what's on your schedule today?" Liz Langley, the owner of the Red Cedar Lodge and Spa asked her husband, Roger, while they were having breakfast.

"I'm off to San Francisco. The partners' meeting is this morning," the handsome middle-aged attorney said. "After that I'm having lunch with Milt Huston and then some more meetings with a few clients I still deal with when I'm in town."

"Hmmmm," Liz said. "That name rings a bell with me. Isn't he some big political deal? Why are you meeting with him?"

"If you consider being Attorney General of the biggest state in the United States, yeah, I'd say he's quite a big deal. He's probably going to be an even bigger deal if he becomes governor next year. I'm meeting with him for just that reason. My law firm is making a large political contribution towards his race for governor, and since I went to law school with him they asked me to personally deliver the check to him. And yes, in answer to your unasked question, I will take another one of those bacon biscuits. Those are delicious."

"Thanks. I serve them a lot to the guests here at the lodge. They love them. Anyway, why do I have the feeling he's pretty controversial?" Liz asked as she passed the biscuits to Roger.

"Because he is. He recently won a major lawsuit on behalf of the State of California against oil companies that were polluting the ground water near their oil operations. It involved illegally dumping toxic oil well byproducts. Sort of like what was in the movie about Erin Brockovich a few years ago. The oil companies are going to have to pay millions, as well they should. Water has always been a critical issue for this state, and even more now that we've been in a drought situation for years."

"Roger, you know I don't have a political bone in my body, but what's the big deal about water? I mean the people in the cities need it, farmers need it, ranchers need it, and a lot of industries need it. Seems to me there's plenty for everybody."

"Fraid not, Liz. There's been a fight over the water rights in our state for longer than we've been alive. The northern part of the state thinks they own the rights to what's collected there, and the southern part of the state feels it should get half of the water no matter where it comes from, since they're part of the same state. Believe me when I say it's been a political storm for years."

"I didn't know that. Do you think Milt can get elected governor because of what he's done with water issues?"

"As far as a political move, I'm not sure it was a smart decision for a man who wants to be governor, but he's a man of integrity, and he acts on what he feels is best for the people of California. He's very liberal, and a lot of people don't like him for that, but on the other hand, a lot of people do respect him for his liberal views. It's going to be an interesting election." Roger looked at his watch and said, "I better get out of here if I expect to make the partners' meeting on time. They don't look kindly on partners who arrive late." He stood up and walked to the door, taking his suit coat with him.

"Winston, keep Liz safe today, and I'll see you tonight," he said as he opened the door and walked out to his car. Winston, Liz's big boxer, sat by her side, seemingly taking Roger's advice to heart.

"Big guy, I think Roger meant to stand by just in case," Liz said.

"I don't think you have to spend the day at my side. Anyway, I have to go into town and get some groceries. Thought I'd stop by Gertie's as well. You can go in with me now that she keeps that special service dog harness for you. I'll get dressed, and we'll be out of here in no time."

As she was getting dressed she looked at herself in the mirror and decided that even though she was in her early fifties, she'd luckily inherited her parents' good genes. Although she'd never been to a plastic surgeon, she'd been sensible about staying out of the sun, and the only lines on her face were laugh lines around her sparkling green eyes. She wore her auburn hair cut short, and it was a perfect frame for her heart-shaped face. She was full-figured, but the fullness was usually described by others as being curvaceous.

An hour later, after Liz had checked the pantry and the refrigerator to see what she needed to buy in town, she said, "Winston, time to go." She carefully stepped around Brandy Boy, the big St. Bernard mascot of the lodge, who was lying in his usual place on the porch waiting until the sun set, and the first guests rang their cottage bell to signal they needed a little nip of the brandy he carried in a cask around his neck. She looked at him and thought, *He's probably the most worthless dog I've ever been around. He does nothing other than lay on the porch all day, but ever since that article ran in the San Francisco paper about his exploits, business has never been better. I'll keep him around for that if nothing else.*

After loading up on groceries at the market and buying dog food for Winston and Brandy Boy at the pet store, Liz headed for Gertie's Diner, intent on treating herself to one of Gertie's famous hamburgers and a malt. She parked in front of the diner and opened the door of her van for Winston, who eagerly ran to the front door of the diner. Gertie, the irrepressible octogenarian owner of Gertie's Diner, had Winston's service dog harness in her hand when Liz and Winston walked in.

With her signature blond beehive hairdo, a pencil stuck behind her ear, bright blue eyeshadow, thick dark red lipstick, and stiletto heels, there was no one else quite like her. Her warmth was legendary, and people came from all around the area to eat and spend a little time with her. She loved her customers, and they loved her.

She adeptly fit the service harness, which she had purchased at a garage sale, over Winston's large chest. "Okay boy, you're legal now. Can't nobody complain 'bout me allowin' a dog in my restaurant since yer' now officially a service dog," Gertie said with a wink directed towards Liz. "And guess what, Winston? Think I saw a big helpin' of steak and eggs sent back to the kitchen. Evidently my new waitress got the order wrong, but that ain't no problem. Purty sure it has yer' name on it. I'll have Ginny bring it out to ya' in a minute."

Liz laughed, "I honestly think he lives for these moments. You're spoiling him rotten, you know."

"With what he did to save yer' life after my brother's murder, it's the least I can do. A little payback time, right Winston?"

The big dog shook his head up and down agreeing with her. Liz rolled her eyes and said, "If anyone overheard this conversation they would think Winston knows everything you're saying."

"Ya' must have missed the memo on that, doll, cuz' he does. To change the subject, I ain't seen my tenant, that handsome husband of yours, around today. He got business in the big city?"

"Yes, he'll be there most of the day. I'm glad he rented the office next to your diner. It's worked out well for him."

"Glad to hear it, honey," she said looking up as the door opened, and a customer walked in. "Gotta go. I'll tell Ginny to get yer' order. Assume ya' want yer' usual burger and malt, and I'll have her bring Winston's out to him too. Tell handsome hi for me," she said with a wink.

"Will do." Liz looked around the diner and smiled at a number of the people who had become her friends since she'd come to the small town of Red Cedar several years ago. It was on the coast about an hour north of San Francisco. She thought how much her life had changed in these few short years. She and her husband, Joe, had bought the lodge and spa hoping it would help him reduce his stress levels and result in better health for him. It didn't, and he'd died of a heart attack not long after they'd moved to Red Cedar.

After Joe died, Liz thought she'd never remarry, but when she met Roger Langley she knew she'd been given a second chance at love and had happily become his wife. She was thankful that the power that controls the universe, whatever it is, believed in giving people second chances. She smiled, reminiscing, as Ginny brought her burger and malt along with Winston's steak and eggs.

She sat for a moment, glad her life was relatively quiet after she'd recently been involved in helping solve several murders. Little did she know all that was about to change.

CHAPTER TWO

When Liz returned to the lodge, she unloaded the groceries and then she and her assistant chef, Gina, prepped as much food as they could for the evening meal Liz served to the guests staying in the cottages at the lodge. She loved to cook for the people who seemed to thoroughly enjoy her food. She'd just told Gina to take a short break before they started the final preparation for the meal when her cell phone rang.

She looked down at the monitor and saw it was Roger. "Hello, sweetheart, how did your meetings go?"

"Well, very well, as a matter of fact one of them went so well we're going to be taking a little trip."

"What are you talking about?" Liz asked.

"Remember how I told you this morning that I was going to meet Milt for lunch and give him a political contribution from our law firm? Well, I did, and he was very grateful. We talked for a while catching up on classmates of ours from law school. Neither one of us is very active as alumnae, but it's always interesting to hear about what some of the others are doing these days. Anyway, his cell phone rang while we were at lunch, and it turned out it was the owner of the Big T Lodge in Texas."

"I've never heard of it. Should I be familiar with it?"

"No, I'm not surprised you haven't heard of it, but anyone who's a duck or quail hunter certainly knows about it. It's probably the most exclusive hunting lodge in the United States. Milt's been going there for years, and he's leaving this weekend for his annual trip to the Big T Lodge. The owner of the lodge had called to tell him that he'd just received a call from a couple who had to cancel their reservation because it turns out their daughter gave birth prematurely, and her husband's in Afghanistan. Naturally, they dropped everything to be with her."

"Okay, but I still don't see what any of that has to do with us."

"Here's the thing, Liz. The owner asked Milt if he knew any hunters who might be interested in taking their places. Milt put his hand over the phone and asked me if I'd like to go. I didn't even have to think about it. I said yes. I've wanted to go there forever, but everyone knows it's almost impossible to make a reservation because it's so exclusive, plus it's terribly expensive. I mean really, really expensive, but here's more good news. The managing partner of the law firm distributed the annual bonus checks today and mine is twice what I thought it would be. It will more than pay for the trip. I know you're not a hunter, but I thought you could relax and might even pick up some recipes from the chef at the lodge. I hear the food is fabulous. What do you think?"

"I think if you're that excited about it, I should get excited too, although this is a world I know nothing about. How many guests will be at the lodge?"

"From what I understand the lodge is quite large and luxurious. I think Milt said last time he went there were twenty guests. Milt told me it's considered to be the best hunting lodge of its kind in the United States."

"Where specifically are we going and when?" she asked.

"We're going to west Texas, and we leave this Sunday. I'll hunt on

Monday, Tuesday, and Wednesday, and then we'll return home on Thursday. When I said we'd go, Milt handed his phone to me, and the lodge owner gave me the airline flight times. He's also sending me a packet of information. All that's left for us to do is make our airline reservations and let him know what time we'll be arriving at the airport, so one of the SUVs from the lodge can pick us up. I'll do that tonight when I get home."

"Roger, today is Wednesday. That sure doesn't give me much time to make sure everything is ship-shape here at the lodge."

"Liz, as well-run as the Red Cedar Lodge and Spa is, I hate to tell you this, but it will run without you just fine. You know Gina can handle the meals on her own, since she's had to do it a couple of times before when you were involved in a murder investigation. Bertha, your lodge manager, can handle everything else, and we'll only be gone for a few days. It's not like we'll be out of touch for a month or more."

"You're right. This will certainly be an adventure, and one I never thought I'd be involved in. What does a well-dressed woman wear to a hunting lodge?" she asked.

"Jeans and boots. We'll know more after I get the packet from the owner. I asked him to FedEx it to me, so we'd have a little heads-up before we leave for the lodge. Anyway, we'll talk more about it tonight. I'm just getting ready to leave the office, so I should be home in about an hour depending on traffic. Liz, I've got to tell you I have never been so excited about anything."

"I'd prefer to hear you say you've never been so excited about a trip. I think getting married should be right up there in your excited ratings," she said drily.

"Well, that goes without saying," Roger said. "You know that."

"Right, Roger, right. See you soon, and yes, I'm excited too."

Liz ended the call and turned to Gina. "Any chance you can come in a little early tomorrow? Looks like I'm leaving Sunday for a hunting lodge in Texas. Never saw that one coming. Anyway, we need to figure out what meals you can serve while I'm gone. I know you can do it, it's just a matter of planning. I'll talk to Bertha in the morning about getting someone to help you, but for right now, let's finish up with this one."

CHAPTER THREE

On Thursday morning FedEx delivered a packet from the Big T Lodge to Roger at his law office in Red Cedar. He called Liz and told her he was coming home for lunch, so they could look at it together. They sat down at the kitchen counter, and he pulled out the contents of the packet. "Liz, I can't believe we're going to this place. Here, why don't you look at their brochure, and I'll read the list of recommended things we should bring."

They were both quiet for a few minutes and then Liz said, "Roger, this is incredible. First of all, look at this photo of the lodge. Even though it' made of logs, the great room is faced in stone and is two stories tall. The picture shows it has a huge fireplace overlooking a lake in the distance. Evidently they have ten duck blinds located near the lake, and the club is situated on 8,000 acres. That's huge. It looks like you'll be hunting ducks very early in the morning, come back for a gourmet breakfast which looks wonderful, change clothes, and go out to the fields for the rest of the day quail hunting."

"Yeah, I agree, it looks fabulous. Looking at this list, I sure don't have the type of hunting gear they recommend I should bring. From what this says I'm going to need specific clothing like neoprene waders for the early morning duck hunting and then a complete change of clothing and regular hunting boots for the rest of the day. One of our clients owns the largest hunting equipment store in San Francisco. I'll call him this afternoon and order what I need to get.

I'll ask him to overnight to me, so I'll have what I need before we leave in a couple of days."

"You might be looking forward to the hunting," Liz said, "but I'm looking at all the dogs and food shown in the photos of the brochure. That's a combination I find hard to resist. I guess you'll be using Labrador retrievers to hunt ducks in the morning and then German short-haired pointers when you hunt quail later in the day."

"There's got to be a huge kennel just to keep all the dogs they must have, plus it says they take you to the duck blinds and the fields in ATVs," Roger said. "That's a lot of dogs and ATVs. No wonder this place is expensive. I'm glad they'll be providing the guns and ammunition. I went hunting with some friends years ago, and registering my shotgun at the airport was a nightmare."

"Roger, won't you need a Texas hunting license?"

"Yeah. I read where licenses can be purchased online when you get there. Think that's what I'll do. They've probably done it a million times, and they'll be able to do it a lot easier than I can. I see that serious look on your face. What's so important?"

"The food, Roger, the food. It says they have a five-star chef. Each guest places their special order for breakfast, so it's not like a buffet. At lunch the hunters eat at dining tables set out in the fields and prior to dinner there's a cocktail hour with appetizers followed by a gourmet dinner. I'm looking at a menu, and I already know one thing I'm going to have."

"What's that?"

"Texas pecan pie. Look at the picture of it. This is going to be some vacation. To change the subject. Will we be traveling with Milt and his wife? I've never met either of them."

"No. His wife isn't going. Her family's visiting from Italy, so she's staying home to be with them. Milt told me it's the first time they've been apart since they were married several months ago. He's flying into Dallas a day early, so he can meet with potential donors."

"That seems bizarre. Why would someone in Texas give money to a man who's running for governor in California?" Liz asked.

"Actually, it's quite common. Often people who live out of state will have business in that state, so they want to grease the palm of the person they think will be in a position to help them. Other donors sometimes think that if a candidate has the potential for a national office, if they make a contribution when he's still holding a state office, that person will be indebted to them in the future. It's a long-term gamble, but it often pays off."

"The political world seems to be a whole different world than the one I'm used to, and one I'm not so sure I'd want to be a part of."

"That it is, Liz, that it is. Now if you'll excuse me, I've got to get back to work."

"Wait, one more thing before you leave. Since I won't be hunting, and I won't need any heavy outdoor type of clothing, I wonder if I need to take something besides jeans and boots?"

"I think you'll be fine with those. I noticed they have a pool, so even though it's winter, you might want to take a bathing suit. And since afternoon rains are pretty common in that area of Texas, you also might want to pack a raincoat."

"I'm about twenty years past sitting by the side of a pool all day even if it is nice, and if it's raining hard enough that I'd have to wear a raincoat, I think I'll stick to the great room with the big fireplace. I'll curl up with a book and be perfectly fine. Actually, I think that's about all I'm going to do while we're there. That and I'll probably spend a little time with the chef, if I can. I'm sure I can pick up some recipes we can use here at our lodge."

"Okay, love, I'm out of here. The bonus I got paid was great, but since most of it will be spent on this once-in-a-lifetime trip, I better get back to the salt mines and earn some money. See you tonight."

The rest of Thursday, Friday, and Saturday went by in a haze for Liz and Roger. He was busy rescheduling clients who had problems that could wait a week and seeing the ones whose issues needed immediate attention. Liz spent a great deal of time with Bertha and Gina making sure that the lodge and spa would run seamlessly during her absence. Saturday night they skipped the regular lodge dinner and packed, wanting to be ready to go the next morning when Hank, Bertha's husband, was scheduled to drive them to the airport in San Francisco.

CHAPTER FOUR

"Thanks, Hank. We really appreciate you taking us to the airport. I still feel guilty about leaving Bertha to manage the lodge and spa on such short notice, but as you know, this came up suddenly," Liz said as they neared the San Francisco airport.

"No problem. I'll help out where I can, but you don't need to worry. Between Bertha and Gina, it will run just as smoothly as if you were there."

"I hope you're not insinuating that I don't do anything at the lodge and spa, and my presence isn't really needed," she said laughing.

"Not at all. By the way, Roger, I've done a lot of hunting over the years, but I've never known you to be a hunter. You got the right boots and everything you need for this trip?"

"One of the firm's clients is Ned Jensen. He's the owner of Jensen Outfitters in San Francisco. I called him, and he put together a bunch of hunting clothes and boots for me. I tried them on, and they seem to be fine."

"Roger, trying them on and wearing them are two different things. I'm going to pull off the freeway at the next rest stop. You need to at least get the boots you'll be wearing all day hunting quail out of your

MURDER AT THE BIG T LODGE

suitcase and wear them today on the plane. Believe me, comfortable boots are the most important thing when you're hunting, but they have to be properly broken in."

"That's a good idea, Hank. I never thought of it. Thanks."

"I wouldn't have either, but a friend of mine had a really rough time once when we were hunting. His boots were brand new, and he put them on when we got to where we were going to be hunting. Six hours later when we got back to the truck he took his boots off, and he'd worn a blister on his foot so bad his heel was bleeding. Matter of fact, after that experience, I always keep some moleskin in the console of my truck in case I go hunting with someone who develops a problem. When we stop I'll get it for you. Keep it on you when you're out hunting. Let's hope you don't have a problem, but it sure is nice to have some with you just in case."

"I probably should have talked to you before I ordered anything. I really appreciate it," Roger said as Hank turned into the rest area and opened the trunk.

A few minutes later when they were back on the freeway Roger said, "These boots actually feel pretty good, but you're absolutely right about breaking them in."

"I may be a country boy, but sometimes us country boys know more than some owner of a hunting shop in a big city. Glad to be of help." A few minutes later Hank said, "Here's the airport. Which terminal do you want?"

"Terminal three. We have a one-and-a-half-hour layover in Denver and then on into El Paso. I understand the lodge is about a two-hour drive from there. Today is one of those grin and bear it travel days. Hurry up and wait. Hurry up and wait."

Hank pulled up to the curb, and they got out of his van. He opened the trunk and the two men took the luggage out of it while Liz stood on the curb with their carry-ons. "Thanks again," Roger said as he and Hank shook hands.

"Happy hunting. I'll pick you up Thursday. Call me if there are any changes, and don't worry about a thing. We'll take good care of Winston and Brandy Boy for you, course, you might have to wrestle Bertha for Winston when you get back. You know how much she likes that dog."

"That I do," Liz said. "Thanks again, Hank. See you in a couple of days."

*****

Several hours later they made their way down the escalator to the baggage claim area in El Paso. At the bottom of it they saw a man wearing cowboy boots and a cowboy hat with a sign that said "Roger Langley." They walked over to him and introduced themselves. Slim, as he asked them to call him, helped them retrieve their luggage, and then he and Roger carried it out to the parking lot.

On the drive to the lodge Liz said, "Slim, I've never been to a hunting lodge before. Can you tell me a little about the Big T Lodge?"

"It's not too far from the Guadalupe Mountain National Park, so even though this part of the country is pretty flat, McKittrick Canyon makes it quite beautiful. Matter of fact, some people stay an extra day just to go sightseein' in the park. Jack Mercer inherited the property from his father, and he's the one who built the lodge and made it into what's considered to be the best huntin' lodge in the United States. He didn't spare money on anything, I'll tell you that."

"How long have you been with the lodge, Slim?" Liz asked.

"Jack finished buildin' it 'bout the time I graduated from high school, so that would be about twenty years ago. He was hirin' people, and I know the land around the lodge like the back of my hand. I've been huntin' since I was big enough to hold a shotgun. He needed guides, and I've been at the lodge ever since. Pays fair, and I like my job. Matter of fact, I'll be guidin' Roger tomorrow."

About two hours later they passed through a huge wrought iron gate with the words "Big T Lodge" spelled out at the top of the gate. "That there's the lodge," Slim said. "It's the buildin' you can see off in the distance. There's a bunch of the other buildins' as well. We got one for the dogs, one for the ATVs, one for the huntin' gear, our bunkhouse, and some small homes for the staff. Take just a couple more minutes to get there."

Liz put her hand on Roger's and said, "This is going to be so much fun. I'm so glad we could do this."

As things turned out, fun, it wasn't. Murder is never fun and having a friend murdered is definitely not fun.

CHAPTER FIVE

Slim drove the big SUV up the curved driveway and stopped in front of the lodge with its large two story front doors made with wood casings and beveled glass. One of the doors had a large inlaid stained glass replica of a mallard duck and the other door depicted a Bobwhite quail in a similar fashion. It was an early winter evening, and the lights from inside the house cast soothing rays of light through the glass doors. The effect was one of total warmth.

Just as Slim reached for the door handle, the door was opened by a tall man with white hair, a plaid shirt, cowboy boots, and the largest silver belt buckle Liz had ever seen said, "You must be Roger and Liz Langley. Welcome to the Big T Lodge. I'm Jack Mercer, the one you spoke to the other day on the phone, and this is Sam," he said, gesturing to the big dog standing beside him. Jack shook their hands and motioned for them to come in. "Slim, take their bags upstairs to number ten." Roger and Liz stepped into the lodge, and Liz looked around in complete amazement.

"This is even more beautiful than the brochure indicated," she said.

"Thanks. Come on, I'll show you the general layout while Slim takes your luggage up to your room. You're the last guests to arrive, and as you can see, some of the them are already enjoying the appetizers and the fireplace in the great room," he said gesturing towards a large fireplace at the far end of the enormous great room located off the entryway.

"Follow me," Jack said with Sam by his side. "The dining room is through this door. Breakfasts and dinners are served in there. Liz, I understand you own a lodge and spa out in California, and since you won't be hunting, you might want to spend some time with Chef Jackson. You're also welcome to walk the grounds. Sam here can go with you. He knows which of the paths are okay for you to take, and he'll physically stop you if you happen to start down the wrong path."

"I'd like that, but he looks a little intimidating. Actually, he looks like a large version of the big boxer dog we have at home. What breed is he?"

"He's a bullmastiff. Got him as a gift from one of the guests a couple of years ago. He's comfortable if I allow someone in the lodge, but he's also very territorial and makes a great guard dog for the lodge and surrounding premises. He gets along fine with the two cats we have on the property, but he's not best of friends with the hunting dogs, so we don't take him out to the kennel. Naturally, since the hunting dogs are just that, they're not allowed in the lodge or on the grounds of the lodge. They have their own fenced-in space, so it's not a problem."

Liz knelt down and put her hand out, so the massive fawn-colored dog could smell her and decide whether or not she was acceptable to him. When he licked her hand, she petted the big dog who looked trustingly up at her with deep dark brown eyes. "Sam, I'm going to be here for a few days, and I'd like to be friends with you. I have to go now, but I'll see you later."

"Interesting," Jack said. "He usually puts up with the guests, but I've never seen him lick one of their hands. He must have decided that you're a special type of dog person."

"She is that," Roger said. "Jack, I think we'd like to go up to our room and freshen up a bit. Even though the flights themselves were fairly short, it's been a long travel day for us what with getting to and from the airports and the layover in Denver. We'll be back shortly."

"Take your time and make yourselves comfortable. You'll see a few of the staff around. If you need anything, ask them. See you later," he said as he turned and walked into the great room to join the other guests. Sam started to follow Liz, but Jack said in a loud voice, "Sam, here." Sam turned around and joined Jack.

"Roger, he never told us where our room is," Liz said as they began to walk up the large curving oak staircase.

"Hopefully, the rooms will be numbered on the outside. Good, they are. Looks like we're down at the end of the hall. Yes, here's the number ten in brass letters, and look, our names are next to the door. After you, my love," he said, opening the door.

Liz walked in and stopped in amazement. She turned back to Roger. "You are not going to believe this. It's not a room, it's a huge suite. Look at that canopied bed. It has to be bigger than a king-size bed, plus the room has upholstered chairs, a chest of drawers, nightstands, and a desk. Wow! And look at this," she said walking through a door. "This must be kind of like a sitting room with a porch outside. The view is absolutely gorgeous. Plus, since we're at the end of the building, they've wrapped the porch around it, and it extends along the side of the building. I may stay here the whole time you're out hunting."

In keeping with the hunting lodge theme, their guest suite had been decorated in tan and grey colors with bright red and green accents. Plaid pillows on the bed complemented the plaid chairs. A green canopy was above the bed. A dark green spread covered the bed and prints of different birds were on the walls which had been painted a soft green with an oak molding surrounding the doors. It was very inviting.

"Yes, you could stay in the room all the time, but I think Sam might be disappointed. Looks like you've already found a friend. I don't remember seeing these rooms in the brochure. There were lots of pictures of quail and ducks, but not rooms. That tells me they're probably trying to appeal to hunters who care more about what they can shoot than where they'll be sleeping at night."

"You're probably right," Liz said. "Come to think of it, I don't know any women who hunt. I did see one woman in that group around the fireplace, but I have no idea if she'll be hunting, or if like me, she's just accompanying her husband. To change the subject, I need to wash my hands. I've been in too many public places today, and the last thing I need to get when I'm on vacation is a cold. Back in a couple of minutes."

Roger was opening his suitcase to retrieve his toiletry kit when he heard Liz exclaim, "Roger, come here. This is just amazing."

He hurried into the bathroom to see what was so amazing. Liz was pointing at a large copper claw foot bathtub positioned in front of a bay window. "Have you ever?" she asked. "I've always wanted to take a bath in a tub like that, and it looks like I'll get my chance now. Plus, I should be able to have a great view of the grounds at the same time. This is sheer decadence, and look at that shower. It's got more jets at more angles than I've ever seen. Slim wasn't kidding when he said the owner spared no expense when he built the lodge."

"Okay, Liz, now that we've seen our room, or suite, let's go downstairs. After our long day, I'd love a glass of wine, ready?"

"After you."

CHAPTER SIX

When they got to the bottom of the stairs and walked into the great room where the other guests had congregated, a man detached himself from the group and walked over to them. He was holding a bottle of red liquid in his hand and a glass.

"Milt, I didn't see you earlier. I'd like to introduce you to my wife, Liz," Roger said. "Liz, this is my friend from law school, Milt Huston." They shook hands. "Milt, I'm sure I'm not the first one to ask, but what in the world are you drinking that's in the bottle?"

"It's something I picked up from the USC basketball team. They've gotten great results from drinking beet juice, so I usually have one at the cocktail hour and another one when I go to bed. I mix it with ground almonds to make it even healthier. I have to say it's really improved my energy level, and when I run for governor that's going to be a big plus. Want to try some?" he asked.

"I would," Liz said. "I've never had beet juice before."

Milt walked over to the bar and got a glass. He poured a little bit of the beet juice in it and handed it to Liz. She took a sip, grimaced, and said, "I think this must be an acquired taste, but thank you anyway."

"Speaking of elections and politics, how was Dallas? Were you successful in raising some money for your campaign?" Roger asked.

"Very. It was far more successful than I'd even hoped. With my recent stand on water issues in California and knowing how important water is here in Texas, I thought going to Dallas might be an exercise in futility."

"That's great. So you're definitely all in for the governor's race?"

"Absolutely. As I told you at lunch the other day, I'm committed to it, but in all honesty, if I found out I didn't have the necessary financial support, and I wouldn't be able to run a very effective campaign, I probably wouldn't run. However, having said that, I think I'll be fine." He turned to Liz and said, "I understand you don't hunt. What do you plan to do during the day while we're out hunting?"

"Nothing more important than reading a book and taking walks," Liz said. Just then she felt something next to her thigh and looked down. Sam sat down next to her leg and looked up at her. She heard Jack's voice calling to the dog, "Sam, come. I'm sorry, Liz, he never does this with guests."

"Jack, I'm fine with having him here. I already miss my dogs, so please, I'd enjoy it if he could sit next to me."

"Well, all right, but you let me know if you change your mind. Now why don't you two come over here and get something to eat and drink. Everyone is way ahead of you and dinner will be served in about half an hour."

Liz walked over to a long table which had several trays labeled "Charcuterie" and then individual small signs in front of them. There was a duck sampler, duck prosciutto with ham, and smoked duck biscuits. She turned to Roger who was pouring them a glass of wine and said, "I've never had any of these things. How interesting." She took a bite of the smoked duck biscuit and said, "This is fantastic. My instincts were right about the food we're going to have during our stay here at the Big T Lodge!"

"Well, sweetheart, your instincts may have been right about the food, but I think mine were right about the wine. Any place that serves Rombauer chardonnay is going to be just fine with me." He held his glass up and said, "To a great vacation." She lightly touched his glass with hers and said, "We made it here, and everything is going to be wonderful."

They spent the next half hour chatting with the other guests. There was the usual: "Where are you from?" "What do you do?" "Have you ever been here before?" It was the type of conversation people have who are going to be spending the next few days together in a special setting.

Their first dinner at the lodge was spectacular, in Liz's view. A few people were beginning to go to their rooms when Roger said, "Liz, I think we need to get some sleep. Tomorrow's going to be a busy day for me, and I want to be ready for it. They're taking us out to the duck blinds before dawn. I'll come back around 9:30 or so, and we can have breakfast together then." With that they excused themselves and made their way up to their room, looking forward to a quiet night's sleep in the middle of nowhere.

CHAPTER SEVEN

The digital alarm clock on the nightstand next to their bed buzzed at six a.m. Liz rolled over in bed and said, "Roger, there must be something about sleeping in a big beautiful lodge out in the middle of nowhere. Honestly, that's one of the best night's sleep I've ever had. I really don't mind waking up early after I've slept so well."

"You're not the only one. I never woke up once. I better get a move on, because I need to put on my gear for duck hunting, and since I've never done it before, I don't want to look like a newbie. All of the hunters are supposed to assemble down in the great room at six-thirty, so I've got just enough time to get suited up."

"I think I'll spend the day reading, taking a walk, and just relaxing," Liz said. "Don't need a lot of make-up and special clothes for that. I'll get dressed and walk you downstairs for your first morning hunt, plus I could use some coffee."

A half hour later they walked down the large curving staircase only to be met by Sam who seemed to have been waiting for Liz. The big dog stood up as soon as she got to the bottom of the stairs and wagged his tail in greeting. "Good morning, Sam," she said. "If I didn't know better, I'd say you might have been waiting for me."

Jack Mercer saw them and walked over. "Have you seen Milt this morning?" he asked. "I'm guessing he overslept. I better go up to his room and wake him up, although usually he's the first one down here in the morning. I'll be back in a couple of minutes."

Jack returned shortly looking grim. "Roger," he said, "would you please come with me?" He turned and walked back up the stairs. Roger shrugged his shoulders as he looked at Liz with a "what's this all about?" look on his face and followed Jack up the stairs.

"I didn't want the rest of the guests to hear this," Jack said as they made their way up the stairs, "but I know Milt's a friend of yours. Unfortunately, he's dead." He opened the door to Milt's room, while Roger stared in shock at his friend who was lying on the bed. A red drink similar to the one Roger had seen Milt drinking the evening before was on the nightstand next to his bed. Roger walked over to the bed and took Milt's hand in his own. There was no pulse, and it was very apparent that Jack was right. His friend, the Attorney General of California, and a candidate for governor of that state, was dead. There were no signs of foul play. It appeared Milt had died of natural causes, even though he was only fifty-three years old.

Immediately Roger thought of the recent death of Antonin Scalia, the Supreme Court Justice. *Good grief, this is just like what happened to him. He died in his sleep in at a Texas hunting lodge.*

"I assume you're going to cancel this morning's duck hunt because of this," Roger said.

Jack looked at him in astonishment, and said, "Are you kidding? Even though the guests are very wealthy, for many of them a trip like this justifies why they work so hard. No, I won't be telling anyone about it. I've decided to say that something came up, and Milt had to leave unexpectedly, which in a way, is true. The hunts scheduled for the next three days will continue as planned. I know Milt was recently married, but I never met his wife. Do you know her?"

Roger was having a hard time absorbing the fact that his host was planning on going about business as usual. He couldn't believe that although his friend had died, his host intended to tell people he'd had to leave unexpectedly. "No, I don't know her," Roger said. "She needs to be notified. Although I'm a lawyer, I have no idea what the law is here in Texas regarding someone dying under circumstances like this."

"I'd appreciate it if you'd call his wife," Jack said. "I really need to get back to the other guests. It's almost time for everyone to go out to the duck blinds. That includes you. Since your wife's staying here, maybe she could call Milt's widow and be here when the mortuary comes to pick up the body. I'll call them now, and they should be here in an hour or so. Matter of fact, I'll talk to your wife and see if she'll take care of the situation." He hurried out of the bedroom and down the stairs.

Although Roger and Milt had never been close friends, and their relationship was more like acquaintances who shared lunch every couple of years, Roger felt very uncomfortable about the way Jack was handling the shocking and sad situation surrounding Milt's death. He wondered if there would be an autopsy, and he certainly didn't feel it was Liz's responsibility to be the one to call Milt's wife and deal with the mortuary, because the owner felt the duck hunt was more important than the loss of a man's life. He walked down the stairs, determined to tell Jack it was his responsibility to call Milt's widow, not Liz's.

When he reached the bottom of the stairs he saw Liz and Jack having an intense conversation off to one side of the great room and away from where the other hunters had gathered as they prepared for the morning duck hunt. When Roger walked over to them, Liz looked at him and said, "Go. I'll take care of this. There's no reason for this to ruin your trip. I wasn't planning on doing anything special today anyway."

Within minutes Jack told the guests the ATVs were in the driveway waiting to take them to the duck blinds. He told them the dogs had already been taken to the blinds and if they hadn't brought their own guns, there were guns and ammunition in the ATVs. The guests hurried out to begin the hunt.

Clearly torn between participating in the duck hunt or staying with

Liz, Roger turned to her and said, "I'm so sorry to involve you in this. I really don't feel good about it, but I honestly don't know what else to do. From what Jack told me upstairs, there's no justice of the peace in this county, and in cases like this, the body is taken directly to a mortuary and then according to Texas law, a county judge can sign the death certificate and release the body to the next of kin. It sure sounds different from the way we do things in California, but I guess this is how it's done in Texas when the death occurs in a rural county with a low population."

"Roger, we both know this isn't the first time I've had to deal with something like this, so try to have a good time. I know that's almost impossible under these circumstances, but there's really nothing to be accomplished by you staying here. I'll take care of it, although I'm certainly not looking forward to making the call to his wife, or I guess I should say widow. I have to tell you the owner of this lodge is pretty far down on my list of what constitutes a decent and caring human being. Do you have Milt's home number?"

"Yes, I have it as well as his wife's name on my cell phone upstairs. I left it on my desk. You'll find it there and again, I'm so sorry you have to be the one to handle this."

"Don't worry about me. I'll do whatever's necessary, and I'll see you when you get back for breakfast. Jack said it would be about 9:30 or so. Good luck duck hunting."

CHAPTER EIGHT

Liz dreaded the thought of having to call Milt's wife. She couldn't imagine someone she didn't know calling her and telling her that Roger had died. She decided to wait until the people from the mortuary came, and she'd be able to tell his wife exactly where his body had been taken.

She shivered involuntarily thinking about the cold-heartedness of Jack, the owner of the lodge. It seemed to Liz the only thing he cared about was making sure the other hunters had a good time and telling them that a guest had died in the lodge where they were staying didn't make for a good time.

The chef's assistant had taken the coffee pot back to the kitchen while the guests were assembling in the hallway, and Liz needed another cup of coffee. Jack had mentioned he'd be in the last ATV to leave, since he wanted to make sure all of the guests had been transported out to the duck blinds. Evidently he'd made a detour to the kitchen, because as she approached the kitchen she overheard him telling the chef and his assistant about Milt's death. He specifically told them not to say anything about the death to the other guests. He wanted everyone to think Milt had an emergency come up, and he had to leave unexpectedly.

Jack told the chef he'd arranged for the mortuary to come and get Milt's body while the rest of the hunters were away from the lodge for the duck hunt, thus making sure that none of them found out that Milt was gone until after they returned to the lodge from the afternoon quail hunt. Liz didn't want to walk into the kitchen while Jack was there, so she decided to forego another cup of coffee and instead, turned and walked into the great room.

It was very clear to Liz she had a new friend, Sam, the big bullmastiff. He hadn't left her side since she'd come down the stairs. Liz wondered if the dog was close to Jack's wife, if he had one. It certainly made no sense for him to have bonded instantly with Liz, however, given what had happened to Milt, she was glad to have his company.

An hour later Liz was in her suite when she heard the doorbell ring downstairs. She looked out the window and saw a mortuary van parked in the driveway. She hurried down the stairs, Sam by her side. The staff employees had all accompanied Jack on the day's hunt, and the chef's assistant opened the front door of the lodge. "Hello, Mr. Gordon, my name is Cassie Sowers. You may remember me from when my husband, Paul, died a few years ago. Mr. Huston's body is upstairs in room number eight. I'll be in the kitchen if you need anything," she said as she turned and walked back to the kitchen.

The man named Mr. Gordon turned to Liz. "Do you know anything about this?" he asked.

"No, not really. My name is Liz Langley. My husband and I are guests here at the Big T Lodge. My husband knew the decedent, actually they'd been in law school together many years ago, but I wouldn't say they were close friends. The owner asked me to call his wife after you got here, so I could give her instructions on how to reach you."

"From what Jack told me on the phone, looks like he died in his sleep," Mr. Gordon said. "I understand he was only fifty-three years old. Seems kind of young, but sometimes things like that happen. Here's what's you can tell his wife. I'll take the body to the mortuary, and then I'll wait for instructions from her. Can't do nuthin' without the death certificate, and since our county's pretty remote, and we don't have a justice of the peace, the judge will probably have to sign it, but I doubt if that will happen until tomorrow.

"When you talk to his wife, tell her not to plan any services or anything for several days. After the death certificate's signed, we'll put him on a plane and fly him out to California, course she'll have to pay the airline in advance." He and his assistant walked up the stairs carrying a gurney. A few minutes later the covered body of Milt Huston was taken down the stairs by them and placed in the rear of the mortuary van.

Mr. Gordon walked back in the lodge and said, "Would you give me a call after you talk to the widow? I'd kinda like a heads-up on what to expect. Here's my business card with my telephone number. I'll convey my condolences when I talk to her. No matter how they die, it's always sad for the ones who are left. Give me about an hour. It'll take that long for us to get back to the mortuary."

"I'm going up and call her now," Liz said. "I'll call you afterwards." The big front door of the lodge closed, and the van drove off while Sam and Liz looked out the window at the long trail of dust it left behind. "Okay, boy, let's get this over with. I have a feeling you're coming up with me again." The big dog walked next to her as she went up the stairs.

Liz dialed the number she'd retrieved from Roger's cell phone and listened to the ringing phone. A moment later a woman's recorded voice said, "You've reached the home of Milt and Valeria Huston. Milt is on a hunting trip in Texas, and I've taken my visiting parents sightseeing in Northern California. We'll be returning in a few days. Our housekeeper is staying at our home with our family pets, but she won't be answering the phone. At the sound of the tone, please leave your message, and one of us will return your call. Thank you and have a nice day," the woman said with an accent that sounded like Italian had been her native language.

"There's no way I'm going to leave a death message on her answer machine," Liz said to Sam. "I guess I'll keep trying every day until I reach her." She looked at her watch and saw that it was too early to call Mr. Gordon. She spent the next half hour unpacking the rest of hers and Roger's clothes and generally getting organized.

CHAPTER NINE

Liz was no stranger to what she called "her niggle," that feeling or little inner voice that always alerted her when something was off, and right now it was making itself heard loud and clear. It was very insistent she go to Milt's room and look around before Roger and the rest of the hunters returned for breakfast. She decided she probably should put Milt's things in his suitcase and have it sent to his wife along with his body. She wished she'd thought to do it earlier and given it to Mr. Gordon when he was here. If anyone questioned why she was in his room, she could use that as an excuse.

She and Sam walked down the hall to Milt's room. She looked up and down the hall and didn't see anyone. *Actually*, she thought, *since all the guests and the guides are out hunting, seems like the only people who are in the lodge right now are Cassie, the chef's assistant, the chef, me. and of course, Sam, although technically he doesn't qualify as a person.*

Liz gingerly opened the door to room number eight, wondering why no fingerprints or any other type of police investigation had been taken. If a death occurred in Northern California, where she and Roger lived, it was normal police procedure for some type of police investigation to occur. She remembered when Barbara Nelson had died in one of the guest cottages at her lodge and the bumbling chief of police, Seth Williams, had looked for evidence of foul play and had dusted for fingerprints.

Of course, that was definitely a murder. This isn't, or so the lodge owner thinks, so I suppose that's why no law enforcement personnel have been called to the lodge.

Her eyes slowly adjusted to the dimness in the room that had been Milt's. She agreed with what Jack had told her. Nothing looked particularly suspicious. She didn't see anything in the room that looked unusual. The bed appeared to have been slept in normally. Evidently Milt had planned on unpacking later, because the only thing that appeared to have been taken out of his suitcase was his dopp kit which was on the bathroom counter. An eye drop bottle was next to it along with a washcloth, a toothbrush, and toothpaste. His clothes were still neatly folded in his suitcase and nothing had been put in the room's chest of drawers or the closet.

Liz put the dopp kit in his suitcase and noticed an attaché case next to it. She looked inside and saw a phone and an iPad. She turned them on and quickly scanned them to see if there had been any recent activity on either one. Evidently Milt had called his wife the evening before as the outgoing telephone number matched the one Roger had given her. There was nothing of interest on the iPad. She put them back in the attaché case.

Sam had been watching her while he was lying on a rug that partially covered the highly polished hardwood floor. She walked over to the nightstand and saw the bottle of beet juice which Milt had evidently put next to his bed along with a glass. The big dog suddenly got up and took a position between Liz and the nightstand, a low growl coming from deep in his throat. He gently pushed her away from the nightstand. She looked down at him. "What is this about, Sam? I just want to look at that bottle." Again, he pushed against her, his nose flaring, and the guard hairs on his back raised.

"Sam, let me look at that bottle. I won't drink from it. Move. I need to get closer."

It was as if the big dog understood every word she said. He slowly moved to one side, and she picked up the bottle. As she did she noticed a strong smell coming from it. She remembered that although

Milt had said he added ground almonds to his drink to make it healthier, she didn't remember the contents of the bottle having such an overpowering pungent smell like the one that was now emanating from the bottle. When she'd taken a sip of the beet juice the evening before, the smell was entirely different from what she now smelled. She screwed the cap back on the bottle, having no idea what to do next.

CHAPTER TEN

Liz quietly closed the door to room eight and walked down the hall to her suite, the bottle in her hand. For some reason, blame it on her niggle, she'd felt compelled to take the beet juice bottle with her when she left Milt's room. She had no idea what she was going to do with it, but something told her it was important that she have it. She sat down at the table in front of the large window that overlooked the well-groomed grounds at the lodge. Sam sat down next to her and looked up, a questioning look in his eyes.

It's almost as if he's asking, "Okay, Liz, now that you have the bottle what are you going to do with it?" She unscrewed the cap and smelled it again. The odor coming from it disgusted her. Once again Sam let out a low growl. The red liquid definitely had a strong smell, but she couldn't identify it.

I don't know anyone in Texas that can help me find out what's in this bottle. I wonder what it is. It sure doesn't smell like beets, and if I'm smelling ground almonds, he must have put an awful lot of them in there.

Liz sat for several more minutes trying to figure out what to do with it. She reached for her cell phone which was on the table and punched in the telephone number for Gordon Mortuary. An almost ghoulish sounding voice on the other end answered and said, "Gordon Mortuary. This is Selene. May I help you?"

The voice sounded like it was waiting for the caller to give directions to where the next dead body was to be picked up, Liz thought. "Yes, my name is Liz

Langley. May I speak with Mr. Gordon?"

"May I tell him what this is regarding?" Selene asked.

"Yes. This is regarding the death of Milt Huston. Mr. Gordon left the Big T Lodge an hour or so ago and asked me to call him after I talked to the decedent's widow."

"Just one moment. I'll see if he's available," Selene said.

A few moments later a male voice said, "This is Stanley Gordon, Mrs. Langley. Were you able to contact Mrs. Huston?"

"I called her, but evidently she's taken her parents, who are visiting from Italy, on a sightseeing trip. The message said she'd be out of town for a few days. I didn't leave a message, because I felt she wouldn't want to hear news like that on an answering machine. I do have a question for you. I have something I'd like to send by FedEx or UPS. Does the town where you're located have a facility that provides a service like that?"

"Yes, you can either go to the post office on Main Street in Riley or go one street over to Elm Street, and there's a private mail box service there that has FedEx. A lot of the ranchers in the area have post office boxes there, because it's simply easier to have their mail sent there rather than to their remote ranches. They generally send in one of the ranch hands several times a week to get their mail. You can easily find it."

"Thanks. Jack said there were several cars available for use by the guests, and he specifically told me since I wasn't hunting, I was more than welcome to use any of them. I think I'll drive into town later, take care of my business at the FedEx store, and then explore the town a little bit. I probably need to pick up some souvenirs from this trip."

"Don't get too excited hoping you'll find things," Stanley Gordon said. "I'd be willing to bet this is one of the smallest towns you've ever been in. There's a grocery store, our mortuary, the post office, the private post office, The Riley Restaurant, and a couple of stores that sell ranch items. Trust me, Dallas it ain't."

"Thanks for your honesty, but I think I'll go the FedEx store anyway. When I finally get in touch with Milt's widow, I'll let you know what she says."

"Good. I'll look forward to hearing from you. Tell your husband I hope he has a good hunt."

"I will," Liz said as she ended the call.

CHAPTER ELEVEN

Liz heard the sounds of the ATVs as they returned the guests to the lodge. She put the bottle of red juice in her suitcase and said, "Come on Sam, let's go greet Roger. I need to get some breakfast."

They'd just reached the bottom of the stairs when Roger walked through the front door. He walked over and hugged her. "How bad was it?" he asked.

"It's been taken care of. I'll tell you all about it later on. I'm starving, and I imagine you are too. How was the hunt?"

"I'll tell you about it over breakfast. Let's go into the dining room." Once they were in the dining room they sat down at one of the tables, and a waiter immediately brought them coffee.

"My name's Jesse," he said. Liz looked up at him and thought how appropriate it was that he was wearing jeans, a button down blue denim shirt and a red kerchief around his neck. Jack had said all of the staff would be at the hunt, so she assumed if he'd been there he must be a great quick change artist.

There was no doubt in Liz's mind they were in the land of cowboys, and Jesse portrayed the look well. He handed each of them a menu and asked if they'd like some fresh squeezed orange juice. They both replied in the affirmative and moments later two chilled glasses of fresh orange juice were placed on the table. "Are you ready to order or would you like a few more minutes?" he asked.

"I think we're ready," Liz said. "I love salmon, and the salmon eggs benedict sounds delicious, but I'm a little concerned about how fresh the salmon is given that we're in a very remote area of Texas."

"Not to worry, Mrs. Langley. Mr. Mercer has it flown in fresh daily. I think you'll be pleased with it."

"I trust your judgment. That's what I'll have. Thank you."

"And for you, sir?" he asked turning towards Roger.

"I've never had venison before. I see you have venison hash on the menu. Do you think it's something I'd like?"

"I can only speak for myself," Jesse said. "It's one of my favorites. It's a traditional type of hash with potatoes, onions, red peppers, and green peppers, but the meat is venison. It's topped with two fried eggs, or you can have them any way you'd like, and it's accompanied by freshly baked sourdough bread."

"You've sold me. I'll take it, but I'd like my eggs poached. Thanks."

"Okay, now that we've ordered, I want to hear all about the hunt," Liz said.

"No, first I want to hear if you were able to get ahold of Milt's widow and if the mortuary people came."

"Not much to tell. I called the number you had on your phone for his wife, but she wasn't there. Evidently her parents are visiting from Italy, and she took them on a little trip. I didn't feel comfortable leaving a death message on her answer phone, so I decided to try again tomorrow. The mortuary picked up Milt's body, and for all intents and purposes, that chapter is closed. Now about the hunt."

"It was very interesting" Roger said. "As you know, we left before dawn. Actually, I would prefer to hunt when it's light. Guess it's having practiced law too long, but I have to admit I was afraid some yahoo would think he saw something and fire his gun in the dark. Anyway, there were two guests plus a guide in each duck blind. The guide uses a duck call to get the ducks to come into our area. The dog that was assigned to our duck blind was a black Labrador retriever by the name of Snoopy. Don't even ask why he has that name. I have no idea. He's there to retrieve the birds, so he lies down on the ground next to the blind while the hunters sit on a bench inside the duck blind."

"So, how does it work?" Liz asked.

"Using his duck call, the guide calls the ducks. All of a sudden there's a bunch of flapping wings and each of us stood up and started shooting. And in answer to your unasked question, yes, I did get a couple. I'd been worried I'd totally embarrass myself, but I made a credible showing. Anyway, when one of us got a duck, Snoopy would hear the splash in the marshy area in front of the blind, and he'd race out and retrieve the duck. Then we'd watch for another flight of ducks, and we'd do it again."

"Okay, it's not my thing, but I'm glad you had a good time. I've got a question. Even though there's a river and a lake, this is pretty dry land. You mentioned a marsh. How can there be a marsh around here?"

"Good question. Jack created it from the lake you see from our suite. It's actually quite a large lake, and at the far end he's built some small dams that make that area kind of like a marsh or a swamp. Jack had ten duck blinds built, all far enough apart from each other to be safe from gunfire coming from a nearby blind. It's really quite an engineering project. Ah, here comes Jesse. I am definitely starving."

Both of them were quiet as they focused on breakfast. Roger was the first to finish. "Liz, why don't you stay here and finish your coffee? I need to go up to the room for a couple of minutes. The quail hunt begins after breakfast, and Jack told us to meet him in the great room when we'd finished breakfast. Sorry for leaving you, but I want to wash up, and I have to change clothes before we take off again. As Jack told us last night, they're serving us lunch while we're out in the field, and then we'll hunt till around 4:30 or so. Try and stay out of trouble, although as big as Sam is and as attached to you as he's become, don't think that's going to be a problem." He stood up from the table and lightly kissed her on the cheek.

"Good hunting and enjoy," Liz said. "You deserve it. I may go into town and see what wonderful things they have, although I've been told if you blink your eyes you'll miss it. Even so, I'd kind of like to get the lay of the land. See you tonight."

CHAPTER TWELVE

During breakfast, Liz decided what she was going to do with the bottle of beet juice she'd taken from Milt's room. She walked up to their suite, Sam beside her, and took her laptop computer out of its carrying bag and booted it up. Moments later she was emailing Sean, a private investigator who was on the staff of Roger's law firm at their San Francisco office. He'd been immensely helpful in providing information to her about possible suspects in several murder cases in which she'd been involved.

In her email she explained what had happened to Milt and about the bottle of liquid she'd found next to his bed. She told him she was sending it to him by FedEx and asked him to have it analyzed. She wrote that Milt had told Roger and her the night before that he drank beet juice with some ground almonds in it twice a day, and he thought he could really feel the benefits. Liz wrote that Milt had offered her a taste of it the evening before, and she'd thought it was horrible. She went on to tell him that the bottle next to Milt's body had an unusual smell to it which she hadn't noticed the night before, and for what it was worth, the bullmastiff who had befriended her growled every time the top was off of the bottle. Liz pressed send, and then she decided to change into some more comfortable clothes before she drove into town.

A few moments later her laptop chimed, indicating there was a message on it. She read what Sean had written.

"Good grief, Liz, you haven't even been there twenty-four hours, and you've already found a dead body? What is it with you? And a bullmastiff befriending you? I've heard of dogs being chick magnets, but I've never heard of someone being a dog magnet, but then again you constantly surprise me. Might want to find out if the dog was ever involved in sniffing out drugs for some government agency like the police or army. Maybe he's onto something.

I'll personally walk it over to the lab as soon as I get it. They're closed today, because the owner had a death in the family, but they should be open tomorrow, and our firm is such a good client, I don't think I'll have any problem getting the analysis to be a priority for them.

I have to tell you I have some concerns about all of this. I knew Milt, and I don't know whether you're aware of it or not, but he was a real health nut. He and I belonged to the same health club in downtown San Francisco, and I don't think I was ever there without seeing him. He was also into eating really healthy food. I remember having lunch with him one time after we played racquet ball, and he told the waiter he was a vegan and didn't eat animal products. He told the waiter to bring him something that would adhere to that. I remember it, because I felt pretty guilty having ordered a steak sandwich with French fries.

If I can get the bottle in question to the lab by tomorrow morning, I should have something for you by tomorrow afternoon. Again, be careful. I know only too well you have an incredible knack for being in the wrong place at the wrong time. Keep that bullmastiff with you. He might be of some help. Tell Roger hi for me."

Liz wrote him back, told him she'd be careful, and thanked him. She wrapped the bottle of beet juice in tissues and carefully put it in her purse, then she walked downstairs to the kitchen. The door to it was open, and she saw a man she assumed was the chef and the woman she had met earlier, Cassie Sowers.

"Hello again, Cassie." She turned to the chef and extended her hand. "Hi, I'm Liz Langley, and I'm assuming from the chef's jacket you're wearing that you're the one responsible for that delicious breakfast I finished a little while ago. I'm really looking forward to the next few days. I own a lodge and spa in Northern California, and I cook the evening meals for the lodge guests. If you have time, I'd love to talk to you about cooking for the guests here at the lodge."

The portly and prematurely grey-haired man in the chef's coat shook her hand and said, "I'm Wes Jackson, and I'd like that very much. I'm sure there's much I can learn from you as well. I'll be here this afternoon, and it's pretty quiet around 1:00 or so. Perhaps we could talk then."

"Wonderful. I'll plan on it. I'm taking one of the cars and going into town. I have something I need to send by FedEx, and I also want to take Milt Huston's attaché case and his suitcase to the mortuary, so they can send it with the body. Anyway, it will give me a chance to see the countryside. Jack told me I could take one of the cars whenever I wanted."

"Yes, that's standard practice here at the lodge, particularly when one of the guests isn't hunting, although that's rarely the case. The keys are either in the ignition or under the floor mat. If you have a problem, let me know, and I'll help you. I see you have a friend waiting for you just outside the door," he said, motioning towards Sam. "He won't come into my kitchen. Actually he likes me, but for some reason he and Cassie have never hit it off. Right, Cassie?"

"Right. He knows I prefer French toy poodles or cats to big old dogs like him. I think there must be something wrong with a dog that looks like a horse. Just ain't normal, if you ask me."

The affable chef laughed and waved goodbye, as Liz walked out of the kitchen.

"Sam, you stay here. I'll be back in a couple of hours," she said as she let herself out through the large front doors of the lodge. The big dog pretended he hadn't heard a word she'd said and followed her out to the car. When she opened the door of the car, he jumped into the passenger seat, ready for riding shotgun into town. Liz laughed to herself knowing there was no way she could physically move the big dog once he'd decided to do or not do something.

CHAPTER THIRTEEN

Liz looked around as she began her drive on the semi-improved dusty road to the small town of Riley, Texas. She saw a few cattle, but mainly the land next to the road on her drive consisted of miles and miles of dry grazing land broken only by an occasional fence constructed to keep the cattle from wandering onto another rancher's land. She saw a few stands of trees that looked like they'd been deliberately planted as a windbreak to protect a ranch house from the fierce winds that occurred from time to time in that part of Texas. From the size of the houses, they looked like they'd probably been built for property managers or ranch hands. She certainly didn't see anything as large and imposing as the Big T Lodge.

After driving for about an hour, she saw a small town in the distance consisting of a few buildings and one traffic light. That was all that made up the small town of Riley, Texas. At the stoplight she made a left turn, then an immediate right turn onto Elm Street, the street Mr. Gordon had told her was where the FedEx store was located. She easily recognized the FedEx logo, told Sam to stay in the car, and walked into the nearly barren office.

She glanced around the stark room and didn't see anyone, so she pushed the red buzzer located on the counter. A few moments later a grey-haired weather-worn woman walked out from a room behind the counter. "Hi. May I help you?" she asked Liz.

"Yes. I have a bottle I'd like to have FedEx'ed overnight. Can you do that? I guess I'm asking if it's possible to overnight something, since this is pretty remote from any major Texas city."

"Land sakes," the woman exclaimed. "You want to pay the FedEx prices to send a bottle of what looks to me to be juice to someone? Whyever for?" She quickly put her hand up to her mouth and then said, "Sorry. Nate, my late husband, always tol' me I asked too many questions, and it ain't none of my business what the customer wants to ship. Shouldn't have asked. By the way, my name is Cindy Lou Larson," she said extending her hand across the counter.

"No problem," Liz replied shaking her hand. "My name is Liz Langley, and yes, I do want to send it. Think it will go out today?"

"Yup, Rod should be here in 'bout half an hour. Since it's got liquid in it I think I better wrap it in bubble wrap. It'll cost you twenty-five cents more. Is that okay?"

"Whatever you feel is the best way to send it so that nothing spills out of the bottle will be fine with me."

"Course I'll have to charge you fer a shipping box as well as the bubble wrap. All together it'll come to $15.95. You'll need to fill out this here address label," Cindy Lou said. "Don't recognize ya' from bein' around these parts, and I purty much know everyone. Might want to put yer' home mailing address on the return address in case somethin' goes wrong."

"Thanks, I will, and no, I'm not from around here. My husband and I are staying at the Big T Lodge. We're from Northern California."

"Lawdy, you must be bucks up to be stayin' at that fancy schmancy place. That's one humdinger of a huntin' lodge 'ol Jack done made fer hisself. Hear it's got antique western furniture in it and a fer real chef. Course that Jack always did have some airs. Guess he's really made a name for hisself if you come all the way out here in the dead of winter jes' to hunt them ducks and quail he plants on his property.

"Never seen the inside of his place. Actually, never been near the property, but I hear it's somethin'. Has special kennels for the dogs and all those ATVs fer takin' the guests out to where they're gonna hunt. Hear he's even got a special buildin' to store the ATVs in at night. Sure am a lotta money to spend jes' to shoot some dumb birds. My ol' daddy used to go out a few miles from here and get all we could eat, and he never had to spend a dime fer them."

When Cindy Lou had finished wrapping the package, Liz paid her and opened the front door. As she was leaving Cindy Lou said, "Nice meetin' ya' Liz. Ya' need anything else, come on back. Like I said, I know purty much everyone from 'round these parts. Even know where a few bodies have been buried."

"Thanks, Cindy Lou. I'll keep it in mind."

There was no one on the sidewalk. The town consisted of only a few buildings, the most prominent one being the Gordon Mortuary. It was a town that serviced the ranch people who lived for miles around it, certainly not tourists. *This is one of the only towns I've ever been in that doesn't even have a T-shirt shop*, Liz thought.

She returned to her car and drove to the Gordon Mortuary. She parked and told Sam to stay in the car. She went into the mortuary, introduced herself to the receptionist, Selene, and left Milt's attaché case and suitcase with her. Liz told her they were the personal property of Milt Huston. She asked Selene to give them to Mr. Gordon, so he could send them with the body when it was transported back to California.

CHAPTER FOURTEEN

When Liz and Sam returned to the lodge, it was early afternoon. She remembered Jack had said in his welcoming speech the night before that the chef always made extra lunches for the guests who chose not to hunt that day. While the lunches for the hunters were quite elaborate and served on portable dining tables set up in the fields near the lake, the lunches kept in the refrigerator at the lodge were also supposed to be quite good. Even though the morning had been emotionally draining for Liz, she realized she was hungry. She knocked on the kitchen door, and a moment later she heard the chef's voice say, "Come in." Sam laid down in front of the door, as Liz walked into the kitchen.

"Mrs. Langley, how was your visit to the fair city of Riley?" Chef Jackson asked.

"Not much to see. I FedEx'ed what I needed to send, and then I decided there wasn't much to see or buy in Riley, so I drove back here to the lodge. I may live in a small town, but I've definitely been to other cities that had a lot more action," she said, laughing.

"Think what it's like for me," Chef Jackson said, wiping his hands on a dish towel. "I studied at the Cordon Bleu in Paris and then came back to the United States and worked in several very fine restaurants. The life I'm leading now is as different from those lives as night and day."

"I must admit I've been curious about why you're working in such a remote place as this," Liz said, as she sat down on a stool at the large kitchen counter.

"I have a long-standing dream of owning my own restaurant. I worked my way up to sous chef at two Michelin restaurants, and some day I'd like to see if I could own a restaurant worthy of a Michelin star. I don't come from a wealthy family. I grew up in Minnesota and consider myself very fortunate to have been able to study in Paris. I met Jack Mercer when I was the sous chef at a very fine restaurant in San Francisco. Jack enjoyed the food so much he asked the manager if he could meet me. We met and talked for a while. I had to get back to work, so he asked if I could meet him when I was finished with work that night. I did, and he offered me the chef's job here at the lodge. He said he had a chef that was very good, but he had a vision of creating a five-star dining experience for his guests.

"He told me he wanted me to create signature dishes that were unlike any other hunting lodge, but still within the parameters of preparing different types of wild game. He pays me a fortune to cook for the hunt guests, and I, in turn, try to come up with unique meals that will be remembered by his guests. I think I've succeeded to some point, because I've been cooking here for several years, and almost all of the guests that are here now are returning guests. Some of them have told me they come back just for my cooking. I don't believe that, but it's nice to hear."

"I'd like to hear more about the guests," Liz said. "Jack mentioned there were always some lunch meals in the refrigerator, and I think I'd like to have lunch now. Is this a bad time for me to be here? Would you rather I take my lunch and eat it elsewhere?"

"No. Actually, this is a good time, and I need a break. I'll join you if you don't mind. It's rare anyone ever comes to my kitchen to eat lunch. The guests feel if they've paid a huge amount of money to come here, they definitely should be out hunting, not talking to the chef in the kitchen. Let me get our lunches, and if you'll allow me, I'll pour you a glass of wine to go with lunch. When I lived in Paris I learned how much better food is with a glass of wine." He returned a few moments later with two plates of food and two glasses of wine.

"This looks interesting. What is it?"

"Well, since this is cattle country, we prepare a lot of dishes that have some form of beef in them. I've prepared a salad with bits of meat in it, but first I made something I've never seen in the United States. It's an appetizer made with elk meat that has been slow-cooked with a sherry-maple glaze. I made the bread this morning, and the wine is a carmenere from Chile. I know American wines are very good, but I think this particular wine sets off the meat perfectly. After all, South America is known for its barbecued meats, and they often drink carmenere wine with them. I didn't think I could improve on the wine selection by serving an American wine."

Liz took a cube of the elk meat appetizer, cut it, and ate it. A moment later she said, "I've never had anything quite like this. It's wonderful, and yes, to my unsophisticated palate this wine is the perfect accompaniment. Unfortunately, we don't have elk where I live, so I don't think this particular dish will be something I could use at my lodge and spa."

"Ahh, that's a pity. It really is such a delicacy your spa guests shouldn't be deprived of it."

"I agree, but I'd like to change the subject. I really would like to hear about the guests who are staying here at the lodge. I'm fascinated that there are so many returning guests."

"Well, as I said, some tell me they return for my food. Many return for the hunts, and I think one or two others return for reasons that have nothing to do with hunting."

Liz looked up from her plate. The little niggle she got from time to time seemed to be telling her that the following conversation might prove very useful in discovering if there was more to Milt's death than simply not waking up after going to sleep.

CHAPTER FIFTEEN

Liz took another bite of the elk meat and had a sip of her wine. She put down her fork and said, "You mentioned there were a couple of guests who might be returning for things other than your food and the hunts. Why do you think they return, if I might ask?"

"You know, I haven't had an opportunity to sit down and talk like this since I don't know when. As a matter of fact, I don't think I ever have since I've been here at the lodge. Like I said earlier, almost all of the guests hunt. Actually, you're the first one who doesn't. I'm sure some of the wives would prefer not to, but they usually hunt to please their husbands and justify the cost of the lodge. Once in a while someone gets sick, but they usually stay in their room, and we take tea and toast up to them or one of the lunches I keep here. Anyway, I probably spoke out of turn, particularly now that Milt Huston is dead. Jack mentioned you were going to help with the mortuary and call his wife," Chef Jackson said. "It really is none of my business, and I don't think Jack would like me telling tales or passing on idle gossip."

"It may be none of your business, but I find it odd that a man in good health, and from what I hear, is an avid health addict, dies in his sleep when he's only in his early fifties. I mean sure, it could happen, but I wonder if there's more to it than that," Liz said. "I'm not satisfied in my own mind that Milt died of natural causes. Don't get me wrong, he very well may have, but on the off chance he didn't, I'd appreciate it if you would tell me whatever you know."

"He certainly was a health addict," the chef said. "He was a vegan, which meant he wouldn't eat any animal products. I always made three special meals for him each day. We even kept the beet juice he made each morning in special bottles in the refrigerator, so he could have a bottle during the cocktail hour and another one when he went to bed. He said it really gave him a lot of energy. I tried it once and practically gagged. I thought it was horrible. Anyway, as much as I like to cook and eat, I could never be a vegan."

"That makes two of us. I consider eating one of the best things about being alive," Liz said laughing.

"I'd like to ask you a question if you don't mind," Chef Jackson said. "Why are you getting involved in this? It seems like you've done what you needed to do, that is, staying here and waiting for Mr. Gordon to take Milt's body to the mortuary as well as notifying his wife. Beyond that, I don't quite understand what it is you want."

"Nor do I," Liz said. "It's kind of strange and certainly nothing I ever set out to do, but in the last couple of years I've helped solve several murders, all of which involved me, my spa, or people I cared about. While it's true I know very little about Milt Huston, my husband went to law school with him and thought he was a very good man. I understand he was quite liberal and had even called a press conference for next week announcing he was going to be a candidate for the office of governor of California."

Liz took a deep breath and continued, "I know this may sound silly, but from the time I was a little girl I had this thing I've learned to call a niggle, for lack of a better word. It's like a little voice in my head that talks to me. It's helped me all my life with things like crossing to the other side of the street before a car jumps the curb, or making sure my car door's locked. In the murder cases I've recently been involved in, each time the niggle has demanded my attention, and I've learned to listen to it. It's been very active this morning. That's why I'd like to hear whatever you can tell me about Milt and the other guests."

Chef Jackson put his fork down and appeared to be deep in thought. Finally, he spoke. "The last two times Milt was here I'm certain he was having an affair with Amanda DeLuise. Her husband, Emilio, likes his drinks and really likes his brandy after the hunt and dinner. He usually stumbles off to bed quite early, and Amanda stays down here and talks to the other guests. Several times I noticed that after Milt left, very soon thereafter she would say good night to everyone and likewise leave. I think what I observed in the past is true based on what I heard last night."

"And what would that be?" Liz asked.

"After dinner I heard angry voices just outside the kitchen. They were coming from the porch. I'm sure I heard Amanda saying 'So you couldn't wait any longer, is that it? I told you I was going to divorce him and then we could get married, but instead you wanted the perfect wife for your campaign, right? You didn't want to have to deal with the issue that you and a divorcee were planning on getting married.' A man's voice who I'm certain was Milt's answered her, 'You got that right. I finally came to realize that the only thing you care about is money, and you knew I'd never have the kind of money Emilio has. I hope you're happy with him. I'm just glad he never found out you were having an affair with me.'

"Amanda answered him and said, 'You don't know that for sure. He very well just might know about it and may want to take revenge against you. Italian men are not known for taking cuckoldry lightly. Anyway, now that you're a married man, it's over. It's one thing for me to have an affair with a single man, but quite another to have one with a married man.'

"The man, who I believe was Milt, answered her with a line I'll never forget. He said, 'Taking a lot for granted, aren't you Amanda? I don't recall ever suggesting we resume our affair now that I'm married, and for the record, now that I'm married, our affair is officially over.'"

"Was that the last thing you overheard?" Liz asked.

"No. I heard Amanda say in a low and very angry voice, 'Merde,' and then it became very quiet. I'm not exactly sure what the word means, but I don't think it's a warm fuzzy word. Anyway, that was the end of their conversation, and they both left the porch. It's none of my business, but it seems to me Amanda might want Milt murdered, because she was so angry and then again, maybe her husband knew about their affair, and only pretended to be drunk. Maybe he wanted to exact revenge on Milt. I don't know. I'm just telling you what I heard."

"Wow! Does Amanda hunt?"

"Amanda does whatever her husband, Emilio, tells her to do. It's a business arrangement, you see. He gets a young attractive wife, and she gets all the money she wants. They came all the way from Italy for this hunt. Evidently he owns a large prestigious winery over there, and his family is very well-respected. His wine is excellent, and he always brings several cases of it when he comes to the lodge. He owns a large private jet, and his pilot flies them here in it. Jack has a private airstrip for guests who have their own planes, and you'd be amazed at how many do." He looked at his watch and said, "I'm sorry. I had no idea it was getting so late. I must begin to prepare things for dinner."

"Chef Jackson, thank you so much for your time and the information. You've given me a lot to think about." Liz stood up and looked around. "There are twenty guests staying here at the lodge, and I imagine all of them will be hungry after today's shoot. I don't see anyone else here in the kitchen. Surely you don't do all the preparations yourself?"

"No. You met my assistant, Cassie, earlier. She spends several hours each day at church. She is a born again Christian and is quite religious. She told me once that religion had saved her life. I don't know what she meant by that, and she's never told me, but I do know she's about the most conservative person I've ever met.

"Cassie also doesn't approve of the wine Emilio brings with him. I think she believes the devil resides here at the lodge because of all the excessive drinking and all the fine food that is served. I don't think she'd be working here if there were any other jobs available in the area. I can't remember whether she's divorced or a widow, but she has to work to support herself. In this part of Texas jobs are pretty hard to come by, and she knows a number of other people would like to have her job, so she continues to work here even though she doesn't like or approve of what goes on here at the lodge."

"One last thing," Liz said. "If she's that conservative, did she ever say anything about Milt? He's certainly got a reputation for being very liberal."

"Yes, he's been here several times, and she ranted and raved to me about how she was very much opposed to his position on abortion and his stand on keeping the Planned Parenthood Centers open. For weeks that was all she talked about. She even made the comment that someday Milt would surely have to pay for the evil he was promoting." Chef Jackson paused and looked at her. "Do you find that significant?"

"Quite frankly, I don't know what to think. At this point we don't even know the cause of Milt's death, and from what Jack told me, since there were no signs of foul play, we may never know. Again, thanks for your honesty. I'm already looking forward to seeing what fabulous things we'll be having for dinner tonight." She put her hand on his arm. "If I do find out anything, I'll let you know."

"Thanks, and if someone here at the lodge was involved in Milt's death, maybe it's the sign I need that I have enough money to take a chance on my dream and open up my own restaurant. We'll see. Talk to you later."

CHAPTER SIXTEEN

After Liz left the kitchen she went up to her suite with Sam at her side. She felt unsettled by the morning's events and decided to see if she could take a nap, hoping it would make her feel better. After tossing and turning with sleep eluding her, she knew that wasn't the answer to making her feel better.

Maybe I need some physical exercise instead of sleep. Jack told me last night there are a number of trails near the lodge and that Sam's very good about making sure the guests don't take a trail that might present some problems for them. He mentioned something about rattlesnakes and armadillos being in the area. I'll definitely pass on both of those.

She laced up her hiking boots and said, "Okay, Sam. Let's see what kind of a tour dog you are." The big dog stood up from where he'd been sleeping next to her bed and walked over to the door, waiting for her to open it.

When she got to the bottom of the stairs she noticed that the kitchen door was open, and Chef Jackson was putting the finishing touches on some pies. "Chef, those look delicious. Are we having them for dinner?"

"Yeah, it's kind of a specialty of mine. They're pecan pies for dessert. I'll put them in the oven just before dinner and serve them warm with vanilla bean ice cream and a molasses bourbon sauce.

They're usually a pretty big hit with the guests."

"I can see why. That's definitely something I'm looking forward to. Jack mentioned there were a number of trails that lead into the area surrounding the lodge. I thought I'd take Sam for a walk. I feel like I need to do something physical."

The chef laughed. "Liz, I don't think you'll be taking Sam for a walk. I think it's more the other way around. Sam will be taking you for a walk. There are a few trails that aren't really safe. Don't think you want a run-in with an armadillo or a rattlesnake. For some reason they tend to favor certain trails. I can practically guarantee you that you'll see some deer and jackrabbits, but they're nothing to be afraid of. If anything, they'll be running away from you. Enjoy your walk!"

"Thanks. I don't know how long we'll be gone, but we'll definitely be back in time for dinner. I wouldn't miss that!"

A few minutes later Liz understood why the chef had said Sam would be taking her for a walk. Several times she'd started to follow a trail only to have the big dog block her way. He was an unmovable mass of muscle, and there was no way she was going to walk down a trial if he didn't want her to. Finally, she decided to simply follow his lead. He walked towards a trail and turned around and looked at her as if to say, "This one's safe, Liz. Come on." The old saying that went something like "When in Rome do as the Romans do" came to mind. Since this was definitely Sam's territory, she figured she'd better do what he wanted her to do.

The trail Sam had chosen for her led away from the barns and the kennels and into a black diamond crape myrtle forest. She imagined it was spectacular when it was fully in bloom. For the first time that day Liz felt like she usually did, upbeat, optimistic about life, and glad to be enjoying some private time with nature. The forest was huge, and as the chef had predicted, she saw some jackrabbits and deer. Sam was very well trained so as not to spook the animals, and he would stand perfectly still whenever he saw one, waiting for it to make the first move.

Liz stopped for a moment and took a sip from the bottle of water she'd brought with her. Sam stopped as well. Liz caught a glimpse of something off to the side of the trail and realized it was a doe with two fawns. They hadn't seen her, so she stood perfectly still watching them, regretting that she'd left her camera at the lodge. A moment later the observant doe spotted them, and the three deer loped off.

Quite a bit later Liz looked at her watch and realized they'd been gone over two hours. She knew Roger would be returning to the lodge momentarily and would probably be worried if she wasn't there. While she'd ambled slowly into the forest, now she quickly retraced her steps on the trail that led back to the lodge. Through the dense cover of the forest she could just make out the lodge in the distance. As she walked towards it she heard a voice speaking not too far from her.

"Rick, trust me on this. Milt Huston is dead. With him out of the way I'm a slam dunk to be governor. I want you to prepare a press release. When I get back I'll call a press conference, and we'll get the ball rolling. I also want you to start sending out feelers for who we want to be on our team. Obviously, I want you to run the campaign. I'll make it well worth your time. You've been lucky for me in the past."

The man who had been speaking was quiet, evidently listening to the voice on the other end of what Liz assumed was a phone that he was using. "How do I know he's dead? He was here at the lodge last night, and then this morning the owner of the lodge, a guy name Jack, announced that Milt had an emergency come up, and he had to leave. When we were walking back to the ATVs after the morning duck hunt, I happened to overhear the owner talking to one of his guides. He said Milt died in his sleep last night, and the local mortuary was coming to pick up his body this morning. He asked the guide to call the chef at the ranch house and make sure the body was gone before he and the guides started taking the hunters back to the lodge for breakfast.

"The body must have been gone because they loaded all of us in the ATVs a few minutes later. We just returned from the afternoon quail hunt, and I came out to the edge of the forest away from the lodge to call you. I didn't want anyone to overhear me talking to you. Here's what I want you to do. Try to nose around a little and see what the word is in Sacramento. Also see if there's any rumor or word on the street that Milt has died.

"I have no idea if his wife has been told. They've only been married a few months. If you don't hear anything about it, might want to tell a few key people that you heard from a good source that Milt is dead. That should start the rumor mills going and prime the pump for my press conference. Look, I've got to go. I don't want anyone to get suspicious about why I'm making a call out here and not in the lodge. I'll call you tomorrow to see what you've found out."

The man talking on the phone was quiet for a moment and then said, "Yeah, I'm pretty stoked. Sure seems like some good karma to me. Milt dying so I can become governor, just like I've always wanted to. Later."

Liz had stepped off the trail and was standing behind a tree, not wanting whoever it was who had been talking to see her. She carefully peeked around the side of the tree and caught a glimpse of a large silver-haired man with a barrel chest hurrying back towards the lodge. She put her hand down and indicated to Sam that he was to stay. She stood there for several minutes, giving the man plenty of time to get back to the lodge.

"Come on, Sam," Liz said. "I've got to get back to the lodge and talk to Roger. Sure seems strange to me that the man I overheard talking on the phone who apparently wants to be governor of California just happened to be here at the lodge at the same time Milt was, and then Milt unexpectedly dies. I don't know, but it all seems a little too convenient."

CHAPTER SEVENTEEN

When Liz and Sam returned to the lodge, she hurried up to her room, hoping Roger had returned. Sam left her and looked for Jack, his inner clock telling him it was time for Jack to feed him his dinner. When she opened the door to their suite she heard the shower running and figured Roger was washing off the dust and grime from the quail hunt. A few moments later he opened the bathroom door and walked out.

"Hi, sweetheart," he said as he walked over and kissed her, "I still feel bad about leaving you to clean up what Jack should have taken care of himself. I know he's supposed to be some big shot in the hunting world, but I think he really mishandled Milt's situation."

"Don't worry about it," she said. I'll tell you everything in a few minutes, and I do mean everything, but I want to hear how your first day as a hunter went. Did you get any quail? And I'm not sure if I'm using the right words."

"You are, and I did. I've owned a shotgun ever since I was a young man. Over the years I've gone out to the local trap and skeet range to practice. I'm actually a pretty good shot. However, this is a whole different ball game. You've got to be ready when the dog goes on point, because everything happens with lightning speed. It was pretty amazing. I was nowhere near the best shot among the hunters, but I did well enough that no one laughed, which I'd been worried about. Now, tell me about your day," he said sitting down in one of the chairs that looked out at the lake.

"I will in a minute, but I'm trying to understand exactly what goes on when you hunt quail. Was it kind of like the duck hunt this morning?"

"Not at all. The quail are in a totally different type of terrain. We went to some open fields where Jack grows feed for his cattle. It was pretty much stubble. Anyway there were two hunters assigned to an area I'd say was about a couple of acres in size. There was a guide who gave the dog we were using, a German shorthair pointer by the name of Baron, instructions. The dog would run back and forth in front of us looking for quail. When the dog scented the smell of the quail he would stop and freeze, pointing his nose at the location where the quail were hidden from sight in the grass. We would slowly and carefully walk to the spot where the quail were hiding. When we got close to them they'd become nervous and would flush and attempt to fly away. That's when we had an opportunity to shoot them.

"When one or both of us shot a bird, the dog would run and bring it back to us. I know it doesn't sound like I did much, but I walked more today than I've walked in a long time, and I'm really tired. Now what about your day?"

For the next hour Liz relayed everything that had happened from the time Roger had left, including her conversation with Chef Jackson, and ending with the conversation she had just overheard in the forest. "Roger, do you have any idea who the man I saw in the forest might be?"

"I'm pretty sure it was Mickey Roberts. Did he have silver hair and a big barrel chest?"

"Yes. The man I saw was a big man with a barrel chest, and I have to say his hair was beautiful. A lot of women my age pay their hairdresser big bucks to have hair that color. I wonder if he dyes it."

"The thought never occurred to me. Jack introduced me to him today at lunch, saying we were both from California, so we should probably get to know each other. I talked to him for a while. He's a California State Senator from Los Angeles, and he's been in politics most of his life. He started out on a local school board and worked his way up from there. Jack told me he wouldn't be surprised if he became the governor of California someday."

"Well, based on what I heard, that certainly seems to be uppermost in his mind. Do you know anything else about him?"

"No, as I said, I'd never heard of him, but other than Milt and my friend Bob, I pretty much steer clear of politics. I will say that from what I've seen of politicians, they often feel that the laws other people have to live by don't apply to them. Remember Richard Nixon? Maybe this is one of those cases, or then again, maybe Milt's death was simply because it was his time. I'll be curious what Sean finds out about the contents of the bottle you sent him. I do wish I'd been a fly on the wall and seen the expression on the clerk's face when you told her you wanted to FedEx a bottle of juice. She'll probably be telling people about that for months to come," he said laughing.

"Roger, this is hardly a laughing matter, and I think you're being a bit insensitive. Anyway, do you have any objections to me emailing Sean and seeing what he can find out about the senator?"

"None at all," Roger said. "While you're at it you might as well ask him to take a look at Amanda and Emilio DeLuise, as well as the chef's assistant, Cassie. If the chef has suspicions, maybe there's something to it. I think we've talked enough about today's events, and I need to get dressed. Don't want to be late for dinner if breakfast and lunch were any indication of what we can expect from the chef."

"Well," Liz said standing up and walking into the bathroom, "If you like warm pecan pie with vanilla bean ice cream and molasses bourbon sauce, I think you'll be happy with tonight's dinner. I'll email Sean after dinner. Give me five minutes to get ready."

CHAPTER EIGHTEEN

Liz and Roger walked downstairs and into the great room where drinks and appetizers were being served. She looked around and realized one of the big differences between California and Texas was in what was being drunk by guests during the cocktail hour. She always served various different kinds of wines to her guests, but here it seemed that most of the guests were drinking bourbon. *Guess it's a Texan thing,* she thought.

She noticed Chef Jackson had prepared a large platter of the elk he'd served her at lunch as well as a platter of other wild game appetizers. She was looking forward to trying the appetizer labelled "Fried Quail in a Pomegranate Raspberry Sauce." Liz was glad to see that the game the hunters shot was being used.

"Good evening, Mrs. Langley, how was your day?" the young man behind the bar asked her as she debated what kind of wine to have. She looked up and recognized the waiter who had served them breakfast, Jesse.

"It was fine, Jesse, thanks for asking."

"What may I get you to drink?"

"Chef Jackson and I had a glass of carmenere at lunch. Do you have any of that?"

"Sure do. It's a big hit with the guests and always goes well with the different meats Chef Jackson cooks. Here you are," he said as he handed her a glass. She took it from him and mentally compared it to the color of the juice that had been in the bottle in Milt's room. The carmenere was a darker red and no odor was coming from it.

"Mr. Langley, what can I get for you?"

"I'd like a bourbon on the rocks. Thanks." Roger saw the shocked look on Liz's face and said, "What the heck? When in Texas I might as well drink like a Texan."

She shook her head and whispered, "You're the one who might just have to pay for it tomorrow."

"Liz, this might come as a shock to you, but I've drunk bourbon a time or two, and I assure you I can handle it. Thanks for your concern though," he said grinning at her.

"Just trying to be your friend," she said. "By the way, you might want to try some of the elk meat. I had some for lunch, and it was wonderful."

A half hour later Jack walked over to the dining room entrance, opened the doors, and announced, "Dinner is served. You'll find a place card with each of your names on it. It's been my experience that if we don't do that, the guests tend to eat with the same people every night, although we do allow married couples to sit together." He nodded towards Liz and Roger as well as another couple who Liz assumed were Amanda and Emilio DeLuise.

Liz and Roger found their places, sat down at the table, and introduced themselves to the six men who were also being seated at their table. A menu of what was going to be served for dinner that evening was at each place. Liz picked it up and knew she was in for another wonderful meal.

Dinner was to begin with a jumbo lump crab cocktail with citrus fruit and a red pepper salsa followed by a hanger steak, French fries, a partially scooped avocado half filled with chilled broccoli cheddar cheese soup, fresh warm rolls, and the pecan pie. *Bring it on,* Liz thought, *after the day I've had, this sounds divine.* A moment later Jesse walked over to their table and served them each a sundae-sized dish full of crabmeat mixed with chopped oranges and grapefruit and garnished with fresh salsa. There was very little conversation while each of the guests savored the crab cocktail.

Liz finished hers and turned to the man seated next to her. "We met briefly, but let me introduce myself again. My name is Liz Langley, and I'm from Northern California. This is my first time here. I'm really impressed with the lodge, and the food here is wonderful. Is this your first time?"

"No, I've been coming here for several years. My name is Mac Ward. I'm from North Carolina, tobacco country," he said with a soft Southern drawl. "If it wasn't for the food, I don't know if I would have kept coming back here, but every time I consider going somewhere new, I remember the wonderful meals Chef Jackson prepares and before you know it, my reservation deposit is in the mail."

"I can certainly understand that. I own a lodge and spa in California and cook meals for my guests, but there's a lot I can learn from Chef Jackson. He seems to be amazingly talented."

"He is. I like it that we can order our own specially prepared breakfast, but I'm fine with the way they serve lunch and dinner. I don't know how he does it, but each year he surprises me. I understand one of the guests who's from your state, Milt Huston, had to leave unexpectedly. Can't say I'm too sorry. I've been here several times when he's been a guest."

"Yes, I understand he had to leave. May I ask why you're not sorry he left?"

Mac put his fork down and looked at Liz with a grim face. "I don't know whether you know it or not, but more tobacco is grown in North Carolina than anywhere else in the United States. Last year an initiative was placed on the California ballot to increase cigarette taxes by $2.00 a pack, but it didn't get enough signatures to qualify. So when the statewide effort failed, Milt started pushing for legislation that would increase the state tax on each pack of cigarettes by $2.00. A lot of other states have been looking to California to see if he'll be able to get the legislature out there to pass it. A number of them intend to do the same thing if it becomes law in California. I understand he's talked to a lot of people in those states and is trying to get them to likewise raise their tax on cigarettes."

"I only met him last night," Liz said, "and I don't smoke, so I'm unfamiliar with the proposed legislation."

"Well, I'm sure you can imagine what will happen to growers like me if it becomes law. It sure would hurt not only North Carolina's tobacco industry, but it would be a huge financial problem for me personally. With all these do-gooders talking about the evils of smoking and how it supposedly causes cancer, cigarette sales have really gone down the toilet in recent years. As a matter of fact, cigarette consumption is at an all-time low. The tax increases enacted in a lot of states are killing my industry. These aren't taxes for generating income. They're punitive taxes to get people to either stop smoking or else not start smoking at all. I hate these do-gooders," Mac said as his face became red with anger. "Add to that a tax of $2.00 per pack, and it will ruin a lot of the smaller growers and sure hurt the rest of us.

"I've often thought it might be nice if Milt had a little hunting accident while he was here at the lodge, but guess since he had to leave that won't happen." He picked up a roll and began buttering it. "Matter of fact, I wrote a letter to Jack telling him I didn't want anything to do with Milt, and to make sure we never hunted together or sat at the same dinner table. Don't think I'd enjoy my food if I had to look at him."

Tell me how you really feel, Liz thought. She wished Roger had been seated closer to her so he could have heard the conversation, but he was across the table engaged in a conversation about the different attributes of hunting dogs.

Fortunately for Liz, Jesse brought the main course, and Liz was able to turn to the man on her right, a retired dentist from Oklahoma, and talk to him during the remainder of the meal. When dinner was finished, Jack announced that brandy would be served in the great room for anyone wanting it and if not, he'd see them in the morning for tomorrow's hunt.

Roger stood up and walked around the table to where Liz was sitting and said, "I'm whipped, and I imagine you are too. I'd much prefer a good night's sleep to brandy. Is that all right with you?"

"Absolutely. It's been a long day and I'm definitely ready for bed."

CHAPTER NINETEEN

"Well," Liz said as she closed the door to their room behind her. "What did you think of dinner?"

"I would come here just for the food. The steak was perfect, and I've never seen lumps of crab that big. I was thinking you could make that salad for your guests. I never would have thought to put cold thick broccoli cheddar cheese soup in a chilled half of an avocado. What was that on top?" Roger asked as he unbuttoned his shirt.

"It tasted like salsa verde. Gave it a nice little tang, and it was really pretty with the garnish of scattered chives. Yes, I could definitely make that at the lodge. I'd give anything if I could make a pie like that pecan pie. It was without a doubt the best one I've ever had."

"Come to think of it, I can't remember you ever serving one. Not your thing?"

"I'd like it to be my thing, but pie crust has an aversion to my hands. I've tried every pie crust recipe in the world, and I have yet to have one even resemble the pie crusts other people seem to be able to make so easily. Mine taste okay, but I'm a firm believer that ninety percent of the appeal of a dish is how it looks."

"Liz, I don't ask for much, but if you could master that pie, I'd be a happy camper."

"You're right. You don't ask for much. I'll talk to Chef Jackson tomorrow. Maybe he can give me some tips. By any chance did you happen to hear any of my conversation with the man sitting next to me, Mac Ward?"

"No, why?"

"Well, I think I've come up with another suspect if it turns out Milt didn't die from natural causes, if you can call a rich tobacco grower from North Carolina a suspect."

"Don't think it matters where someone is from or what they do for a living. Crime seems to cut through all of it, although we do need to keep one thing in mind. We're making a lot of suppositions that Milt was murdered. So far we don't have a shred of evidence to support that claim."

"That's true, but I want to be prepared just in case Sean gets back to me with an analysis from the lab that indicates there was something in that bottle that caused Milt's death."

"Probably not a bad idea. Now tell me what makes you suspicious of the tobacco grower."

She told him about her conversation with Mac Ward and how the more he talked, the angrier he seemed to get. When she was finished Roger said, "When I had lunch with Milt last week, he mentioned he was really taking a strong stand against smoking. He felt that public sentiment would be with him during his campaign, since so many people have either died from cancer caused by smoking or know someone who has cancer. He also mentioned that years ago no one would have ever thought that smoking would be banned in restaurants and bars and other public places, and now it is. He felt it was a sign that the United States, and particularly California, was ready to go to the next level, the $2.00 per pack cigarette tax."

"Who knows, maybe Mac thought he'd be doing the tobacco

industry a favor by getting rid of Milt. Of course that's just a hypothetical thought of mine at the moment," Liz said.

"You're right sweetheart. That is definitely just a hypothetical thought. So if Sean comes back with something, then what? Let's see, you've identified Mickey, Amanda, Emilio, Cassie, and now Mac as possible suspects. If, and I repeat the word if, Sean's friend at the crime lab determines there was a substance in the juice that resulted in Milt's death, what do you intend to do about it?" he asked in a teasing manner.

Liz stood at the window and looked into the darkness as if searching for the answer. Finally, she turned around and looked at Roger who had gotten into bed. "Roger, I honestly don't know. Go ahead and turn out the light. I'm going to send an email to Sean. I'll go in the other room, so I won't disturb you. I'll be in bed in a few minutes."

She sat down and composed an email to Sean asking him to find out what he could about Mickey Roberts, Amanda and Emilio DeLuise, Cassie Sowers, and Mac Ward. She wrote what she knew about each of them and concluded the email by telling him she realized Milt might very well have died from natural causes, but even so, she was still curious about those people based on what she'd learned today. She thanked him for helping her and told him that Roger said to bill the firm for his time and charge it to Roger's account.

Exhausted she closed her laptop and got into bed, snuggling close to the warm sleeping body of her husband.

CHAPTER TWENTY

The next morning Liz stayed in bed while Roger went on his early morning duck hunt. When she heard the ATVs return, she went downstairs to join Roger for breakfast. At the bottom of the stairs Sam was wagging his tail and waiting for her. "Good morning, Sam." His whole body shook with happiness when he saw her. Roger saw Liz, walked over to her, and gave her a friendly good morning kiss.

"Roger, I'm not sure I've ever seen a dog this big be able to wiggle his entire body like Sam does. It'd probably be great on YouTube." Sam laid down at the entrance to the dining room, one huge paw on top of the other, his large head resting on them, all the while watching Liz.

"Good morning, Mr. and Mrs. Langley. May I bring you some coffee?" Jesse asked as soon as they were seated.

"Please, and as you might remember, we both take it black. Thank you," Roger said as he eyed the menu. "I will probably really regret this, but I can't pass up crème brulee French toast. As a matter of fact, I don't think I've ever had it before. I may not pass this way again, and I'd really regret it if I didn't try it. What are you having, Liz?"

"Lemon soufflé pancakes with fresh blueberry syrup. That sounds decadent and delicious, but don't get any ideas about me making them when we get back home. The way we're eating, we're both going to have to do some serious dieting and exercising."

"Speak for yourself, woman, but I'm out there all day walking in the fields. I'm sure I'm burning up more calories than I'm taking in," Roger said.

"Uh-huh, you wish," Liz said. "Keep believing that until you get on the scale when we get home. Actually, maybe we should hide the scale. Might be better for our psyches."

A few minutes later Jesse returned with their breakfast orders and served them. "I'm not big on people taking pictures of their food before they eat, but this is one of the few times I wish I'd brought my iPhone down with me, so I could discreetly capture this moment. These are both simply beautiful," Liz said, staring at the two plates of food.

"I agree. I don't know what that chef gets paid, but whatever it is, he's worth it."

"Actually, in the conversation I had with him yesterday, he led me to believe it was quite a bit, but I agree, he's definitely worth it. Wish I could afford to have him work for me at the Red Cedar Lodge."

"Well, since you can't, think you better get some recipes from him. This is every bit as good as it looks," he said after his first bite.

"Ditto," Liz said.

*****

After Roger had left for the rest of the day to hunt quail, Sam followed Liz up to her room. She called Milt's home number again, on one hand hoping to reach his widow, but on the other hand wishing she wouldn't answer the phone, so Liz wouldn't have to deliver the devastating news to her. This time a soft female voice with an Italian accent answered the phone. "Hello," she said.

Liz took a deep breath and said, "May I speak with Mrs. Huston?"

"This is she," the soft voice said. "How may I help you?"

"Mrs. Huston, we've never met. My name is Liz Langley. My husband went to law school with your husband, and we are at the hunting lodge in Texas where your husband came."

"I'm confused. I believe my husband is still there," the soft voice said. "Has something happened to Milt?"

"I guess there's no way to tell you this but straight out. I am so sorry to be the one to have to tell you that your husband died in his sleep night before last. There is no evidence of foul play. I am so sorry. I called yesterday, but you were with your parents on a trip, and I didn't want to leave this message on your answering machine. Are they still with you?"

There was a long pause for several moments, and then Liz heard the sound of a primal scream followed by hysterical sobbing. A man's voice came on the phone and in a heavy Italian accent asked, "Who is this, and what did you say to my daughter?"

"My name is Liz Langley. I am so sorry. I'm at the hunting lodge where her husband came. He died in his sleep the night before last. As I told your daughter, I tried to reach her yesterday, but evidently you were all on a trip. I'm glad you're there with her."

"Where is Milt?" the man asked.

"His body was taken to the Gordon Mortuary in Riley, Texas. It's about sixty miles from the location of the Big T Lodge where Milt was staying. The owner said he would personally see to it that Milt's body is flown back to Sacramento. He asked that Mrs. Huston call the mortuary to work out the details. I put Milt's personal effects in his suitcase and delivered it and his attaché case to the mortuary. They'll be sent to you as well. Here's the number of the mortuary. Again, I am so sorry."

"I must leave this call. I need to take care of my daughter. I can't believe this. Milt was just about the healthiest person I've ever known. This can't be. What you don't know is my daughter just found out she's pregnant. Milt not only left her, he left his unborn child as well. She was going to call him tonight and tell him the wonderful news. This is a tragedy. Goodbye."

When the call ended, Liz stared out the window, thinking of the cruel twist of fate that had ruined a woman's happiness. She wondered again if Milt's death had been caused by murder. She picked up a book she'd brought with her, hoping to lose herself in the story until she heard from Sean.

If the liquid in the bottle has nothing to do with Milt's death, I'll just have to accept it as one of those cruel and horrible things that sometimes happens in life. However, if there was something in it, and if Milt was murdered, I'm going to do everything I can to find the murderer for the sake of that unborn child, Liz vowed.

CHAPTER TWENTY-ONE

Liz thought it was rather ironic that she'd decided to bring a murder mystery book with her, but after she started reading it, she quickly became immersed in the fast-paced story line and before she knew it, the morning had almost slipped away. She'd been subconsciously waiting to hear the ping on her laptop computer which would let her know she'd received an email and when she heard it, she hoped it would be from Sean. She quickly stood up from the club chair she'd been sitting in and walked over to look at her laptop which was on a nearby table.

She looked down at it and saw there was an email from Sean. She sat down and began to read it. The email from him was very long, and Liz had to read it several times to absorb what he had written.

"Liz, if you decide to get out of the lodge and spa business, you can always get a job with me working as a private investigator. I had the bottle of juice analyzed, and your instincts were absolutely right. The odor you smelled came from potassium cyanide, which is known for its strong almond smell. It's a deadly poison. That's right. Milt was definitely poisoned. I know you said that Milt put ground almonds in his beet drink, but they wouldn't smell that strong. I don't know what you want to do with this information, but I would suggest you talk to Roger. Remember, he's a very good criminal attorney, and unless the laws have changed in the last few minutes, murder is definitely a crime, although they may play it a little differently back there in Texas.

As to the cast of characters you inquired about. Let me begin with Mickey Roberts. Since he's a politician, I found pages and pages of articles about him. I spent some time reading them, and it boils down to this. He's a very aggressive politician whose main goal in life is to be elected governor of California. As far as scandals, there have been a couple. He's never been convicted of anything, but he's skated on thin ice a couple of times.

He was fined by the Fair Political Practices Commission for money laundering. His laundering scheme consisted of having a number of his wealthy donors contribute money to the Los Angeles County Democratic Party. The money they contributed was earmarked by both Roberts and the party to be spent by the party on his re-election campaign. That's strictly against the ethics code, however, he was only given a slap on the wrist in the form of a $10,000 fine, which is peanuts to a California Senator.

The second scandal occurred when he was accused by an opponent of not living in the Senate district he represents. This is a practice a lot of politicians use. They say they live in the district, so they can establish residence in the district, but in reality it's just an address and is usually a small apartment or even an empty house. In his case he rented a condominium which he didn't live in, but claimed it was his residence, however there were pictures of him going in and out of the large house where he actually lives in Beverly Hills. His neighbors all knew him and said that when he wasn't in Sacramento, that's where he lived. Several articles I read hinted that he may have paid off someone, because the problem went away. Maybe he paid off his opponent, but it became a non-issue in his last campaign.

So in summary, here's what I found out about this guy. He plays hard and fast with the law, and it looks to me like he thinks he's above it. From everything I read, he's politically very aggressive and currently is very focused on becoming the next governor of California. Do I think he's capable of murder? If something or someone stood in the way of his goal, I think there's a good chance he could commit murder. How? I don't know. If all the guests had rooms in the lodge, it probably wouldn't be too hard to sneak into the room of another guest. Guess you'll have to figure that out, but be careful."

Liz stood up and walked over to the window and looked out at the lake, thinking about what she'd just read. There was plenty more in Sean's email about the other people she'd asked Sean to investigate for her, but she needed a few moments to think about the man named Mickey Roberts. If he was the one who murdered Milt, he certainly would have known Milt was dead, and the conversation she'd overheard out in the forest may have been a total lie. He might never have heard Jack say anything about Milt's death.

Several minutes later she walked back to the table where her laptop was and sat down. She looked at the screen and read "Liz, the only thing I could find out about the woman named Cassie Sowers was that she lived in Riley, Texas, and had once been married. Evidently her husband died. Sorry I can't be much help to you about her. Maybe there's someone you could talk to in Riley that could help you.

Yes, Sean, there certainly is someone I can talk to. Cindy Lou at the FedEx office would probably know something about Cassie. She seems to know everyone who lives in these parts, and if anyone knows something about Cassie, I'd bet it's her. I'll go there this afternoon and see what I can find out. Now, back to his email.

CHAPTER TWENTY-TWO

Liz looked down at the screen to see what else Sean had written.

"Amanda and Emilio DeLuise are interesting people. Emilio met her when he went to Napa, California, for a wine conference several years ago. Her family owns a boutique winery in Napa, and she attended the conference. I can only assume that one thing led to another. She's quite a bit younger than he is, probably by at least thirty years. He's sixty-one. From the photographs I saw of her, she's stunning. Anyway, he went back to Italy and divorced his wife of thirty-three years.

It was quite the scandal given that his vineyard is one of the largest and most respected in Italy, and the family is so well-known. Plus, there's the Catholic angle. Usually men in his position in Italy don't divorce their wives. They may have a mistress, but the church doesn't look kindly on divorce. Emilio was evidently quite generous in his gifts to the church, and his marriage was annulled. How a marriage can be annulled after thirty-three years, and when there are three adult children from it, mystifies me. I guess his gifts to his church over the years helped.

It seems Amanda may have looked outside her marriage for a little fun. There were many articles hinting she'd had liaisons with a number of different men, in fact, one even hinted that Milt Huston and she met at a hunting lodge in Texas and continued their relationship from year to year.

From what I read, Emilio is also known for his temper. There's a reference to him being responsible for the death of the son of a neighboring vineyard owner. Evidently they were both in love with the same woman. She's the one Emilio was married to for all those years. He was never prosecuted, and there were hints that law enforcement officials were paid off. Every article says he's devoted to Amanda, and that several times angry words have been exchanged between him and other men when Emilio felt the men were getting too familiar with his wife. She travels with him wherever he goes, so if she is having affairs, she must be a master at finding the time to get away from him in order to conduct them.

Lastly, he's known to love the grape. One article said something to the effect that it was a good thing he owned a vineyard, or he'd be bankrupt from buying the amount of wine he consumes. Could he or Amanda have murdered Milt? Possibly. Amanda may have been furious that Milt had gotten married and that he'd told her he no longer would be having an affair with her. On the other hand, Emilio could have found out about their affair and decided to kill Milt. If you haven't talked to either one of them, might be interesting to see what they have to say, but you're the one who's so good at sleuthing. Be curious what you find out.

Now to Mac Ward. He's an interesting man. His family has made a fortune over the years from farming tobacco. He has more acres planted in tobacco than any other tobacco farmer in North Carolina, and he's passionate about tobacco farming. He's declared publicly many times that there is no correlation between lung cancer and smoking. He completely denies the possibility that there's even a nexus. Mac has smoked since he was twelve years old, and he believes everyone should start at a young age. It's rather amazing given all the evidence to the contrary that he's turned such a blind eye to the problems that come from tobacco, but obviously it's in his best business interests to do that.

Over the years he's gone head to head with different organizations and elected officials concerning the use of tobacco. I found several articles about how much he hated Milt Huston and his proposed legislation which would add an additional tax of $2.00 to each pack of cigarettes. They've been on opposing sides of debates throughout the country regarding the subject of the cigarette tax. Mac is the number one spokesperson and go-to person in the United States when it comes to the subject of being pro-tobacco.

"The most recent article I read speculated on what his reaction would be if Milt was able to get legislation passed calling for an additional $2.00 tax and what would happen after it was passed. The author theorized that it might be the end of the tobacco industry in the United States. Would Mac feel threatened enough to take matters in his own hands? Maybe.

Liz, that's all I could find, but think there's plenty of meat there for you to chew on. If anything else comes up, I'll let you know. If you find out something about Cassie Sowers, I'd like to know.

As always, be careful and give my best to Roger."

Liz looked at her watch and saw that she'd spent over an hour reading and thinking about Sean's email. She decided to go down to the kitchen and see if Chef Jackson would be willing to tell her how to make the pecan pie they had last night for dessert. While she was there she could see what was for lunch and then she wanted to go to Riley and talk to Cindy Lou.

CHAPTER TWENTY-THREE

Liz and Sam walked down the stairs, but as he had been trained to do, Sam laid down in front of the open door to the kitchen. "Good afternoon, Chef. I'm wondering if you have a couple of minutes to talk to me."

"I need to take a break so, yes, I can certainly make time for you. Are you having any luck discovering what happened to Milt Huston? And secondly, may I interest you in some lunch and a glass of wine?"

"Lunch sounds wonderful. What fabulous thing have you come up with today?"

"There was some leftover ham from a dinner I made last week. I froze it and then defrosted it today. This is a new dish for me, so you can test it. I plan on making a panini type of sandwich with the ham, an Asian sweet sour sauce, grilled onions, and brie cheese. How does that sound to you?"

"Since my mouth is already watering, it's telling me it sounds divine. Sounds like an interesting combination of flavors. What type of bread do you plan on using?" Liz asked.

"I thought it would go well on rye bread. I'll make the sandwiches for us, and then I'd really like your opinion."

Liz sat down at the counter while he assembled them. "Chef Jackson, I have a number of questions for you. First, I'd like to know if there is any way you could tell me how to make the pecan pie we had for dinner last night. I'm a good cook, but pies don't seem to like me. Do you have any tips?"

He turned away from the range where he was grilling the sandwiches and said, "Liz, I can't tell you how many people have said that to me. Actually, I got the recipe from someone who had tried for years to make a good pie, and the recipe spells it out with all the tips you'll ever need for getting the crust perfect. I'll make a copy of it for you. It explains everything far better than my words could ever do. Would that be all right with you?"

"That would be more than all right. My husband told me if I could learn to make that pie he would be happy for the rest of his life, or it certainly sounded that way to me."

"Not a problem," he said as he plated the sandwiches and reached into the refrigerator for two fruit compotes. "Thought we needed something to cut the heaviness of the sandwich, and I think fruit will go well with them. And of course we need a glass of wine to launch the inauguration of my new sandwich."

"What ae you serving me today?" she asked.

"I thought this pinot noir would go well with it. It's a light red wine and not too heavy. Try it and see what you think."

A few moments later she said, "The sandwich is fantastic. I've never had anything quite like this and I agree, this wine complements it perfectly. I definitely think you should serve this as a meal, although I know the guides prepare meals tableside for lunch, and the guests probably don't want a sandwich for dinner. I'll just consider myself very lucky for not going hunting. Thank you so much. It's definitely something I'll make for my husband when we get back to California."

"Thanks. Now let's get back to Milt. It may sound weird, but my mother always said I had a gift for knowing when people had more to say than they let on. I can't explain it any other way, but I'm definitely getting the feeling you've found out something about Milt's death. Would I be right?" he asked.

"Maybe we're kindred spirits. As I told you yesterday, I always get a niggle that lets me know when something isn't quite right. Yes, I do know more about his death. No one has told me not to say anything, and there's no reason why I shouldn't, but it would make me feel better if you'd assure me that this conversation remains between you and me for now."

"You sound very serious, Liz. Yes, I promise you I won't repeat anything you tell me."

CHAPTER TWENTY-FOUR

"Liz, before you start, I'd prefer it if you'd call me Wes from now on. Chef seems a little too formal if you're going to be sharing secrets with me."

"All right, Wes, I don't think these are secrets, but as I said, I would like to keep what I'm about to tell you confidential. As a matter of fact, I'm not real sure what they are. Let me start from the beginning. My husband is a partner in a large law firm in San Francisco. One of the top private investigators in the United States works for his firm, and he's been very helpful to me in the past. I think I mentioned I've been involved in helping solve several murder cases in the past. Sean, that's the investigator's name, has become not only a friend, but a go-to person when I'd like to get some information about something or someone."

"Let me interrupt, Liz, but as far as I know there is nothing that points to Milt being murdered, so I'm a little unclear as to why you're telling me this."

"I'm not very proud of this, but yesterday when everyone had left for the duck hunt, and Milt's body had been taken to the mortuary, I went into his room. I wanted to pack up his clothes and personal effects and send them to his wife, which I did. While I was in his room, I saw a bottle of red liquid next to his bed. It looked like the same bottle I'd seen him drinking from the night before during the cocktail hour. Actually he wasn't drinking directly out of the bottle. He poured the contents of the bottle into a cocktail glass and then drank it. Milt told Roger and me that it was beet juice, the miracle juice that the University of Southern California basketball team drinks before every practice and every game for enhanced performance. He said he felt it really worked for him."

"I know he drank beet juice. I think I even mentioned to you that he used to prepare two bottles in the mornings, and we'd refrigerate them for him. He'd always have a glass of it during the cocktail hour and another one when he went to bed," Wes said.

"When I went into his room Sam was with me. There was a very strong smell coming from the bottle which was sitting on his nightstand with the top removed. I walked over to it, and Sam stood in front of it as if to block me from getting it. I told Sam I wasn't going to drink it, but I simply wanted to look at it. I swear the dog understood, because he moved away. I don't know why I took it, but I did. You may remember I went into town yesterday. Well, I took it to the FedEx store and sent it to Sean. I wanted him to take it to a crime lab he uses and have it analyzed, which he did." Liz sat back and looked Wes directly in the eye.

"Milt was murdered. Sean sent me an email this morning which said that large traces of potassium cyanide, a deadly poison, were found in the liquid that was in the bottle."

Wes was quiet for several moments and then spoke. "Liz, my mind is whirling. Let me sort out some of my thoughts by verbalizing them. First of all, Sam very well might have known there was a poison in the bottle. Jack told me once that he got Sam from a guest who worked for a drug enforcement agency. Sam had been highly trained, but he refused to lie down on command, and if a dog fails that test, he can't work for the agency. The guest thought Sam probably didn't feel in control when he was lying down. The guest wasn't sure what he was going to do with him, and Jack told him he'd been thinking of getting a guard dog for the lodge, and he'd like to take him.

"Secondly, and what really concerns me, is that the murderer must be someone here at the lodge, either a guest or an employee. Is that what you're thinking?"

"Unfortunately, yes. In the short time I've been at the lodge I've discovered that several people here could possibly have been responsible for Milt's death. At least they certainly qualify as suspects, because each of them appears to have a motive for wanting him dead. I sent their names to Sean, and here's what he had to say about them."

She spent the next half hour telling Wes what Sean had found out about Mac, Amanda, Emilio, Mickey, and Cassie.

"Amanda and Emilio I've already discussed with you," Wes said. "Yes, either one of them could have reason to murder Milt. You remember the conversation or rather, the argument, I heard hours before Milt was murdered. They certainly would seem to qualify as suspects."

"That's what I thought, too," Liz said. "Something else I remember reading is that women murderers tend to use poisons and things of that nature rather than guns or knives. If that's true, Amanda may possibly be the murderer."

"I don't know. If she wasn't going to leave her husband for Milt, that's a big risk for her to take just because the affair had been terminated by Milt. I find it hard to accept. She would have an awful lot to lose if she were caught."

"That's true, but revenge is a powerful motive, and from what you've told me about her and what Sean sent me, I don't think she would like to be told that a man was no longer interested in her."

"I've always wondered about Emilio," Wes said, "and whether his love of the grape wasn't overstated. Yes, he always had brandy after dinner, sometimes several, but he's a big man, and owning a vineyard, he may simply have developed quite a capacity for alcohol. He could have feigned drunkenness, gone up to Milt's room, and put potassium cyanide into the bottle of beet juice sitting on the nightstand."

"Certainly he's a suspect, but let's talk about Mickey. Is there anything you can add to what Sean found out? I understand he's been here several times before. What's your impression of him?" Liz asked.

"I can't tell you much. He struck me as a typical politician, glad-handing everybody, and trying to ingratiate himself with everyone, hoping, I suppose, to get a political contribution. He's likeable, but a bit too smarmy for my taste."

"Did you notice whether or not there was much interaction between Milt and Mickey? I would almost think there would have had to have been some, given they were both in politics and from the same state. They must have known each other."

"Liz, I don't go on the hunts, since I'm here in the kitchen all day cooking the meals and overseeing the kitchen activities. I really don't see much of the guests. They could have talked and had dinner together, but that's strictly conjecture on my part."

"Since Milt usually came at the same time every year, at least that's what I'm inferring based on his affair with Amanda, that would mean Mickey would have known when he was going to be here."

"Yes, that's true, but there's another way he could have found out. Jack has quite an ego, and he's really into status and money. On his website he lists who the guests are and when they will be at the lodge. He's very careful to put something next to each of their names that indicates status or money, such as so and so is a state senator or the owner of the largest tobacco farm in the United States."

"What you're telling me is that anyone could have looked at the website and discovered when Milt was going to be here. Am I right?"

"Yes, Liz, that's exactly right. Something else that probably needs to be talked about is why Mac would come when Milt was here.

From what you've told me and also from what Jack has said, Mac hated Milt. Don't you think it's interesting he'd choose to come here when Milt was scheduled to be here? Maybe he came here at exactly this time so he could murder Milt and hopefully have his tobacco problems go away."

CHAPTER TWENTY-FIVE

Wes stood up from the table where he and Liz were sitting in the lodge's kitchen and poured himself a glass of water. "Would you like one?" he asked.

"No thanks. Let's talk about Mickey Roberts. I think he's a very strong suspect. With Milt out of the running, Mickey immediately becomes the frontrunner in the race for California governor. Mickey had to know that Milt would be a very formidable candidate and would have the money to spend to get the word out that Mickey has a couple of unsavory things in his past. It seems like all of these people have, at least in their minds, a reason to want Milt dead, but I think Mickey might have the most to gain from his death. Wes, I just thought of something else concerning Mickey."

She told him about overhearing Mickey's phone conversation with someone named Rick and how Mickey had said he knew Milt was dead, because he'd heard Jack ask a guide to call the lodge and make sure the mortuary had taken the body. "Wes, did Jack or one of the guides call you regarding the removal of Milt's body by the mortuary?"

"No. I never got a call from Jack that morning. I suppose Cassie could have picked up the phone if I was in the restroom or something, but that's doubtful. I think she would have mentioned it. She pretty much worships Jack. Liz, based on what you're telling me,

I agree with you that Mickey had a lot to gain from Milt's death. Let me change the subject. You said Sean couldn't find out anything about Cassie other than the fact she'd been married. I don't understand why you even asked him about her. She's simply my assistant."

"That may be true, but you did tell me she was furious about Milt's stand on the Planned Parenthood Clinics. Was she furious enough to kill him? It's not the first time someone has been killed over the abortion issue. What do you know about her?"

"Quite frankly, not a lot. When I came to work here several years ago I obviously needed to hire someone to be my assistant. I wanted that person to do the prep work, like chopping and getting the ingredients ready for me, so I didn't have to bother with that stuff when I began to cook the meals. You know, the time-consuming stuff. They didn't have to be a chef. There's a newspaper in the area, The Riley Times, that comes out twice weekly. I posted an ad in it for a chef's assistant. Several people answered the ad, but Cassie was the only one who had experience working in a kitchen. There's a little diner in town, and I mean little, but it does a fair business, because it's the only one in town. Cassie had been working there for several years. That's why I hired her."

"How has she been as an employee?"

"She does what I tell her, and that's really all I expected from anyone I hired. I didn't plan on my assistant coming up with gourmet creations. She does her job well enough that it frees me to be creative, which is what I wanted."

"What do you know about her personal life?" Liz asked.

"Not much. We don't have the kind of relationship where we tell each other what we did the night before or things like that. It's pretty much a straight up business relationship. I don't think she's ever taken a sick day or missed work because of personal reasons."

"Evidently she's a widow and has two children. Do you know

anything about her deceased husband or her children?"

"No. Wait a minute. I did have each of the people who applied for the job fill out an application. There's a large pantry behind the kitchen, and my desk is located there. I'll be back in just a moment."

He returned with a completed job application form in his hand. He sat down and looked at it. "It looks like her husband's name was Paul Sowers, and she has two grown children by the names of Megan and Chris. Hmmm, this is interesting. On her application she wrote that her husband was deceased. For some reason, I thought she was divorced. Guess not."

"Did she write anything of a personal nature?"

"Not a thing. That's it, sum and total. There's nothing on it other than her work background and things like her address, etc."

"May I see it? I think I'll check out her address. I want to go to town and see if the woman who works at the FedEx, Cindy Lou, knows anything about her."

"Sure," he said, handing the application to her. She took it from him and wrote down the address.

"Liz, while we've been talking I've also been thinking, and quite frankly, I'm not sure how I feel about what I'm thinking."

"I'm sorry, Wes, but that makes absolutely no sense to me. Can you spell it out for me?"

He stood up and started pacing back and forth. "I could lose my job over this, but I know where the master key is to all the guest rooms. I don't know how you're going to find out who did this, but maybe there's some evidence in one of the suspects' rooms. What do you think?"

She looked at him incredulously. "You're asking me if I want to go into the rooms of the various different possible suspects and search them without their permission? Do you know what could happen to me if anyone finds out? I don't want to even think what Roger might say about this."

"Roger wouldn't need to know, and if you don't want to do it, I completely understand. I just thought it was a way for you to possibly get more information."

"I may regret this the rest of my life, but I think I would like to do it. I probably better do it right now if I'm going to do it, or I'll lose my nerve. Anyway, everyone's gone, so it probably is the best time. Are you coming with me?"

"I know this sounds like an excuse, but I really do need get things ready for dinner. I'm afraid you're on your own for this."

"Thanks," she said sarcastically. "I guess I'm the fall guy here. What time do you expect Cassie back?"

"She should be here within the hour. She's here for breakfast, and then she's off for several hours. She returns in the afternoon to help with dinner. I believe I mentioned to you she's quite religious. I think she spends her time off at church."

"Actually, that will work out well. I'll go up to the rooms now and then drive into Riley. I'd like to drive by Cassie's house and get a sense of it after I talk to Cindy Lou. Show me where the key is. By the way, do you have any plastic gloves? And if not, plastic wrap will do fine. I don't want to leave any fingerprints, although from what I've seen, I don't think anyone around here has fingerprinting equipment."

"Let's hope it never comes to that," Wes said motioning for Liz to follow him. They walked into the pantry, and he pointed to the wall where a key on a chain hung from a peg. "Stay here while I get the plastic gloves for you. I'll be back in a minute."

"Hurry up, Wes, or I'm going to lose my nerve."

A few moments later Wes returned with the gloves. "Good luck. Let me know what happens."

"I don't want anything to happen. I want to find evidence that someone murdered Milt. One last thing, if someone comes back early could you do something to alert me?"

"Sure. I'll take a large metal bowl and drop it on the floor. That should make enough noise that you'll be able to hear it. With everyone gone it's pretty quiet here. Okay?"

"Yes. Wish me luck," she said as she put on the gloves and took the key from him. "Glad that Jack has the name of each guest posted next to their room. At least I won't have to waste time trying to figure out who's in which room."

"Well, as they say on Broadway, break a leg," Wes said.

CHAPTER TWENTY-SIX

As soon as Liz walked out of the kitchen she was joined by Sam. She looked around the downstairs portion of the lodge to make sure no one had returned unexpectedly from the hunt. Not seeing anyone, she breathed a sigh of relief knowing she had the whole upstairs to herself on this, her first-ever time of committing the crime of breaking and entering.

She wasn't sure what she should even look for. Since there wasn't a murder weapon, per se, she decided to look for anything that could relate to Milt. The first room she entered was Amanda and Emilio's. It was perfectly clean as Jack had two cleaning ladies come in each morning as soon as the guests left for the duck hunt. The rooms were clean by the time they returned from the hunt.

Liz looked through the closet and glanced through their suitcases. She didn't find anything, nor was there anything in the bathroom. If Amanda had been having an affair with Milt, Liz doubted there would be anything about him in Amanda's personal items. She gingerly went through Emilio's briefcase and found only items relating to the vineyard and winery he owned in Italy. She looked at her watch and realized she'd used up fifteen minutes of the hour before Cassie was to come back to the lodge. Although there was no reason for Cassie to come upstairs, she knew she'd feel better if she could finish her search before Cassie returned.

The next room she entered was Mickey Roberts' room. There were a number of papers on the table that served as a desk. She began to go through them and realized she was looking at the campaign timetable for Mickey and how he planned to spend the next few months. His laptop computer was on the table, and she opened it. It immediately booted up, needing no password. What popped up on the screen was an email from a man she presumed was his campaign chairman, Rick, evidently the man Mickey had called the previous day regarding Milt's death.

In his email Rick indicated he hadn't found anyone in Sacramento who had heard of Milt's death, but that he'd been able to hire a number of the top campaign workers as well as the campaign consultant that Milt had used for his previous campaigns. Rick said all of them would need proof of Milt's death, but if it was true, they were ready to go forward with his campaign for governor. He ended by saying it looked like the campaign would be a slam dunk for Mickey, and now they wouldn't have to worry about anyone else having the political clout or the money to seriously oppose Mickey.

None of that particularly surprised Liz based on the phone conversation she'd overheard him have with Rick. He remained a top suspect in her mind for two reasons. First, with Milt dead, he was in a very good position to be the next governor of California. Secondly was the disturbing thought that if Mickey was the one who killed Milt, he would know that Milt was dead, which meant he'd never overheard Jack asking his guide to call the lodge to see if Milt's body had been removed by the mortuary. Since Wes had told her he'd never received such a call, although it wouldn't stand up in a court of law, to her it seemed that Mickey easily could have been the murderer.

Liz quickly went through the stack of papers on the table. About halfway down were a number of articles about Milt as well as a printout of the dates that Milt was to be at the lodge. Once again, while it wasn't proof that Mickey was the killer, it was one more thing that pointed in that direction. She wished she could find the tipping point. The rest of her search was fruitless, so she walked down the hall to the third and last of the suspects' rooms, that of Mac Ward.

Liz and Sam quickly entered the room, closing the door behind them. She spent several minutes looking through his clothes and other personal effects. She found nothing. She opened the drawer of the table that also served as a desk and saw an iPad in it. She pulled it out and turned it on. There was a long email from a man who she assumed, based on the content, was a tobacco farmer. She scanned it and saw that it was about an article the man had seen in a North Carolina paper regarding Milt's proposed cigarette tax increase.

The man was extremely upset, saying that it could be the beginning of the end of tobacco farming. He concluded his email by telling Mac he hoped Mac would take the steps necessary to do whatever needed to be done to stop Milt from having the legislation enacted. She heard a car door slam and looked out the window. Cassie had returned. Liz put the iPad back in the drawer, quickly left the room, and rapidly walked down the hall to her suite, her heart pounding. After she was safely in it, she took several deep breaths to calm herself. She sensed Sam's concern and patted him on the head, "It's okay Sam. We made it just in time."

Well, from what I found it looks like either Mickey or Mac could have been the murderer. I certainly saw nothing that would indicate Amanda or Emilio had anything to do with it. She looked at her watch. *Perfect, I have just enough time to drive to town and get back before Roger returns from the afternoon quail hunt.*

Liz walked downstairs with Sam at her side and knocked on the kitchen door. Wes opened the door. "Wes, Sam and I are going into town. We should be back before the hunters return. See you later." He had an inquiring look on his face. Without saying a word, she handed him the key and gave him a thumbs up.

CHAPTER TWENTY-SEVEN

When Liz got to Riley, she noticed a small building with the words "The Riley Restaurant" printed on the front window. She assumed this was the little diner Wes had told her about, the one where Cassie had worked before he'd hired her. Liz had a hard time imagining the small little building being a restaurant and was surprised that whoever owned it hadn't just called it The Riley Diner.

I'd really like to go in there and see what the restaurant is like, but I don't have time if I'm going to get back before Roger and the rest of the hunters return to the lodge. He gives me pretty free rein when I'm involved in things like this, but I don't want to push my luck. I definitely don't think he'd approve of my room investigation.

She parked in front of the FedEx office and walked in, the overhead bell ringing. Once again, she was the only customer in the office. Cindy Lou heard the bell announcing the arrival of a customer and walked through the curtain that separated the back room from the office.

"Well, what a surprise! You bein' here two days in a row. Got another bottle of somethin' you want to spend your money shippin' somewhere?" she asked laughing. "Busts me up every time I think 'bout hard-earned money used to ship a bottle of juice by FedEx, but guess the customer is always right. Leastways, that's what I've been tol'. What can I do fer ya' today, darlin'?"

"I'm not shipping anything today, Cindy Lou, but I have a question for you. You told me if I needed to know anything I should talk to you, because you know pretty much everyone around here. I'm curious about a woman who works at the hunting lodge named Cassie Sowers. Can you tell me anything about her?"

"Maybe I can, and maybe I can't. Why do ya' wanna know?"

Okay, Liz thought, *don't really like to do this, but I have a feeling I'm being told she might tell me something if I offer her money. She hasn't said anything, but my niggle is up, and that's what it's telling me.* Liz opened her purse, took out a $50.00 bill, and laid it on the counter.

Cindy Lou looked at the money with a shrewd look in her eyes. "It must be important to you, if yer' willin' to spend a Uly on it. Don't see too many of them hereabouts."

"It is, and I am," Liz said, pushing the $50.00 bill with the face of Ulysses S. Grant on it across the counter. Cindy Lou appeared to be having a war of ethics waging within her, but she finally took the bill, folded it up, and put it down the front of the checkered red and white blouse she wore.

"Okay, now that we got that lil' chore outta' the way, what do ya' want to know 'bout Cassie?"

"Anything you can tell me. I'm particularly interested in her husband Paul. How did he die? He must have been very young."

Cindy Lou didn't say anything for a few moments, and then she began to speak, "Kinda go fer the meat, don't ya', girl?"

"I have no idea what you mean."

"Lots of what I'm gonna tell ya' is rumor. Seems like Paul had himself a lil' chicken on the side, if ya' know what I mean. Heard the lil' chicken done come up with an egg in her one day that was gonna be hatched in a few months. Cassie heard 'bout it and danged if Paul didn't up and die in his sleep. Then a funny thing happened. Chicken died in her sleep, too. Lotta folks around here thought it were some kinda weird coincidence, I can tell ya' that, but weren't no signs of foul play or nuthin', so the sheriff said it was just a strange happenin'."

"I'd say that's a very strange happening," Liz said.

"Think one of the things that saved Cassie was that she got religion right after that. I mean I ain't never seen no one get religion like that girl did."

"In what way?" Liz asked.

"Well, she told people God visited her right after 'the incident' as she called it. There's a little fundamentalist church right outside of town, and she started attendin' it. Actually, that's not the right word. She pretty much lived there when she weren't workin' at The Riley Restaurant or at home with her kids. When they finished high school they moved out and went to El Paso. Cassie did whatever Reverend Benson wanted her to do, and it seems like Billy Bob kept her right busy. From what I hear she still spends most of her time there, and it's been quite a few years now. Her kids are long gone, so yeah, it's been a long spell since it all happened."

"Cindy Lou, this may sound like a strange question, but do you have any idea how Cassie feels about abortion?"

"Don't take one of 'em Rhodesian scholars or whatever they call 'em to answer that question. All you gotta do is go out to her house and take a look-see through her windows. Ever bit of wall space in that dang house is covered with posters protestin' abortions. Matter of fact, every time one of them abortion doctors gets hisself shot and killed, she makes copies of the newspaper article and passes it out to people. Guess that all comes with her gettin' religion."

"Thanks Cindy Lou. I really appreciate the information. I'd like to ask a favor of you."

"Shoot, darlin'."

"I'd appreciate it you would keep this conversation just between the two of us. Could you promise me that?"

"Sure. That's the least I can do when somebody gives me a Uly. You and I ain't never had this conversation."

"Thanks again. By the way, Cassie's house sounds pretty interesting. Where does she live?" Liz asked.

"Take the main road out of town in the other direction from where you came in and follow it down 'bout three miles. You'll see a mailbox with a straggly rose planted next to it and Cassie's name on the mailbox. Turn into the lane, and within a few yards you'll be there. Gotta tell ya' it's a far cry from where yer' stayin'.'"

"What do you mean?"

"Jes' go out there and see fer yerself. Her old house looks like the flip side of a coin from The Big T Lodge. Jes' be a little careful. If'n Lex, that pit bull she has, ain't chained up, probably don't wanna go in her yard. Coupla people still have scars from that cur. Ya' be careful."

"Thanks, I will. I have a healthy respect for dogs off leash," Liz said as she walked out the door and got into the hunt club's car.

She turned to Sam and said, "I want you to stay in the car and behave yourself if you see Cassie's dog. If the dog is off leash, I'll be staying in the car with you."

CHAPTER TWENTY-EIGHT

As she began the drive to Cassie's house, Liz checked her odometer. When it showed she'd gone three miles she saw a mailbox with a scraggly rose bush next to it. She slowed down and checked the name on the box. Just as Cindy Lou had said, the mail box was Cassie's. She turned into a gravel lane and was glad she'd seen Cassie go into the lodge earlier, so Liz knew she wasn't home.

Liz saw a house up ahead about fifty yards. Cindy Lou hadn't been kidding. The front yard, if one could call it that, was covered with brown stubble. If there had ever been grass, it had been replaced by weeds long ago. The small brick house had been severely neglected. Paint was peeling off of the front door and shutters. The two steps which led up to the front door were badly cracked and had weeds growing out of them.

She stopped the car and rolled down the window. Liz heard the sound of a large dog barking furiously, but she didn't see one at the fence at the rear of the house. She gingerly got out of the car and walked over to the fence. The barking seemed to be coming from a small detached garage next to the house.

Whew, she thought, *Cassie must have locked the dog up in the garage.* She looked around to see if there was anyone nearby. Satisfied she was alone, she walked over to the front window and looked in. She gasped with astonishment. Every square inch of wall space was plastered with posters such as "Save Our Children" and "A Fetus Is a Living Thing," but what really caused her concern was the large poster behind the couch in the living room. Evidently Cassie had taken a photo of Milt Huston and had it enlarged. White concentric rings had been painted on Milt's upper torso with a red bull's eye over the center of his chest. Liz was mesmerized and frightened, both at the same time, as she stared through the window at the bizarre scene in front of her.

She took her phone from the pocket where she'd put it and photographed the poster with Milt displayed on it. She couldn't wait to show Roger the photograph she'd taken. It didn't mean Cassie was the one who murdered Milt, but it sure made a case that she could have been the one who did it. Cassie was now definitely at the top of Liz's list of possible suspects. Liz decided she'd spent enough time at Cassie's house, and she didn't want to have to answer a nosy neighbor's questions about why she was there, so she turned around and headed back to her car. Once she was in her car, she made a U-turn, and drove back down the gravel lane that led to the highway.

So Cassie's husband died under suspicious circumstance and so did his lover, the chicken, as Cindy Lou called her. Now a guest at the hunt club where Cassie works also dies under suspicious circumstances. Sure sounds like a lot of strange circumstances. I wonder if Stanley Gordon from the mortuary in Riley knows anything about those two deaths. I have to go through town on my way back to the lodge, so I might as well stop by the mortuary and see if he can tell me anything.

A few minutes later Liz pulled into the Gordon Mortuary parking lot. There were two parked cars in it. She hoped one was Selene's, and that the other one belonged to Stanley Gordon. When Liz entered the mortuary she saw Selene sitting at her desk. "Hi, I don't know if you remember me, but I brought some things in yesterday to be shipped to California with Milt Huston's body. I was wondering if Mr. Gordon is in, and if so, if he could spare me a moment of his time."

"I'm sure he can, Mrs. Langley. As a matter of fact, Nick, one of the employees here, just left for El Paso. He's putting Mr. Huston's body on a flight that leaves for California late this afternoon. His widow's father called and made the arrangements. I'll tell Mr. Gordon you're here." She called him and then said, "He'll be happy to see you. His office is through that door."

Liz knocked on the door, and it was immediately opened by Stanley Gordon. "I understand one of your employees has taken Milt's body to the airport in El Paso to be flown to California," she said. "I'm glad that's taken care of. I spoke with his widow this morning, and she was devastated. Her father got on the phone and told me she was pregnant, but Milt didn't know about it. She was going to tell him about it tonight."

"I am so sorry. Having a loved one die is tragic enough, but a circumstance like that makes it even worse. My heart goes out to her."

"Mine too, but that's not the reason I'm here," Liz said. "I was talking to someone who told me that the husband of a woman who works at the Big T Lodge, Cassie Sowers, died several years ago. This person also told me that evidently her husband had been having an affair with a woman who died about the same time. Both of them died in their sleep. I'm wondering if you handled the funerals or if the families used your mortuary."

Stanley looked at Liz for a long time and then said, "That's a very odd thing for a stranger like you to ask about. Why do you want to know?"

Liz wondered how much she should tell him and then realized that sooner or later the cause of Milt's death would be made public. That being the case, she decided to tell Stanley everything she knew. She took a deep breath and began. She told him about finding the liquid in Milt's room, how she had it analyzed, her suspicions about some of the guests, and then what she had just seen at Cassie's home.

Stanley sat quietly and listened as Liz talked, his fingers steepled under his chin, his elbows on his desk. His grey hair was thinning, and that, along with his rimless glasses and large paunch, made him look like the quintessential small town mortuary owner.

When Liz was finished he sat for several moments seemingly lost in thought, and then he began to speak. "Yes, my mortuary was where both of those bodies were brought. There were no signs of foul play on either of them, but something didn't seem right to me. I remember thinking at the time that I wished we had someone here locally who could conduct an autopsy and a lab that could analyze the contents of their stomachs. I suspected that both of them had been poisoned, but as you know, in rural counties like ours when there's no sign of foul play, a judge signs the death certificate, and that's that. He never has to even see the body. That's what happened in both of those cases."

"How well did you know Paul and the other woman?"

"I'm about twenty years older than they were, so I'd have to say I'd known them all my life. I've also known Cassie all her life. I always wondered if Cassie had something to do with their deaths. It was just too coincidental. Cassie really changed after that. I don't know if you heard, but she became extremely religious, actually a zealot, although Billy Bob, the pastor at her church doesn't mind much, because she really helps him. I always wondered if Cassie's sudden conversion to becoming a religious fanatic had something to do with their deaths, but I couldn't prove it. Cassie never pursued finding out the cause of their deaths, and the other woman, whose name was Julia Walker, didn't have a family. She lived by herself, and one of her neighbors noticed her blinds were drawn for several days, which wasn't normal. Her neighbor was the one who discovered her body, so there really wasn't any reason to do anything. Seemed like no one cared."

"Stanley, if you don't mind, I'd like your opinion on something. Do you think Cassie is capable of murdering someone?"

"I don't know. The person I knew when she was younger, no. The person she's become, possibly. Now let me ask you something."

"Of course," Liz said.

"What do you intend to do with this information?"

"I don't know. I'd like to know if her husband, Paul, and the woman named Julia were poisoned, but I don't know how that can be done."

"Actually, I might be able to help you," Stanley said. "Both of them are buried in the Gordon Cemetery. According to Texas law, if someone has knowledge or suspects that someone was poisoned, the sheriff has the authority to order that the body be exhumed and examined by a forensic medical pathologist. It seems to me there's sufficient evidence concerning Milt's cause of death that the sheriff might be willing to make such an order. He's a very good friend of mine. I'd like to tell him what you've found out, if that would be all right with you."

"Yes, sooner or later the truth about Milt's death will have to be told, although I don't think Jack will be very happy about the fact it occurred at his hunting lodge. If it's determined that Paul and Julia were poisoned, there would be a nexus to Cassie, although how that could be determined I'm not sure. How long would it take? I rather doubt there's someone qualified to conduct a forensic examination of the two exhumed bodies from around here."

"That's true. The sheriff would have to request that someone from El Paso come here to Riley to conduct the examination. Actually, it could probably be done tomorrow if I call him now, but I'm concerned about one thing."

"What's that?" Liz asked.

"Cassie comes to the graveyard every day and puts a flower on Paul's grave. She's been doing that since the day he was buried, even in the worst weather imaginable. She's obviously going to find out his body has been exhumed for one reason or another. If she suspects that your information had anything to do with it, and if Cassie is the murderer, you could be in danger. I just want to make that clear to you before I place the call to the sheriff."

Liz sat quietly for several moments. "I see what you're saying, but sooner or later she's going to know I was involved when the sheriff makes it known I was the one who discovered that Milt's death was caused by a fatal dose of poison, not from dying in his sleep."

"Liz, my family has been in this business for several generations, and I take this profession and my title as owner of the Gordon Mortuary very seriously. I have no choice, given what I now know, but to request that the bodies of Paul and Julia be exhumed and examined. Failure to do so would be unethical. However, I also feel this is your decision, because you're the one whose life may be in jeopardy. I want you to be very sure this is what you want me to do."

"Stanley, I don't think I could live with myself if I had knowledge that there's a good chance two people were murdered, and I chose to do nothing with that information. I promise I'll be very careful. As a matter of fact, if you look out the window, you'll see a huge dog in the car I'm driving that's kind of adopted me. He's with me during the day at the lodge, and my husband is with me at night. Thanks for your concern, but I'll be fine. Go ahead and make the call to the sheriff while I use the bathroom."

When she returned Stanley said, "I talked to the sheriff, and he said he'd arrange for the bodies of Paul and Julia to be exhumed tomorrow. He's having a forensic pathologist come and examine the bodies and test them for the presence of any poison. He said he'd make it a top priority, and we should have the results late tomorrow or first thing day after tomorrow. I just want to tell you how much I admire you for doing this, but again, I want to caution you to be careful. I know there are a lot of guns at the lodge, but do you have your own?"

"No. I have one at my home in California, but there certainly didn't seem to be any reason for me to bring it on this trip."

He stood up and walked over to a glass gun case at the rear of his office. He took a keychain out of his pocket and opened the case. A moment later he walked over to her and said, "Take this gun. It's small, and I'd like you to keep it with you at all times. I'm assuming you know how to shoot a gun, right?"

"Yes. There have been several times when my husband insisted I carry one with me. I'm no stranger to them, and I really appreciate your concern. Thank you, but isn't there some requirement that I need to have a license to carry the gun?"

"No, here in Texas our gun laws are very liberal and almost nonexistent. It's perfectly legal under Texas law for me to give the gun to you and for you to carry it. There's no need for registration or anything like that."

"Again, thanks. Here's my cell phone number," Liz said. "When you learn something I'd appreciate it if you'd call me."

Stanley stood up and put his hand out. "Trust me, you'll be the first to know anything. You're a very brave woman. Tell your husband he's a lucky man."

"Thanks," Liz said smiling, "although there have been times when I'm not so sure he'd agree with you." She shook his hand and walked out to her car where Sam was patiently waiting, the late afternoon sky beginning to turn grey, the forerunner of the night sky.

CHAPTER TWENTY-NINE

When Liz returned to the lodge she was glad she had about half an hour before the hunters would be returning. Sam followed her to the kitchen and laid down in front of the door. She knocked on it, and Wes immediately opened it. "Come in, Liz. I've been thinking about you. What did you find out this afternoon?"

She looked around the kitchen and whispered, "Where's Cassie?"

"We have a little building close by where we keep our non-refrigerated items. I sent her over there with a long list of things we need. I was hoping she'd be there when you returned. She won't be back for a half hour or so. If you can kind of summarize what you found out, I'd appreciate it, because I'm a little under the gun this time of day."

"I'll make it quick and simple." She briefly told him what she'd found when she'd searched the rooms, her visit to Cindy Lou, and concluded with the revelation that the bodies of Paul and Julia were going to be exhumed.

He stared at her for a moment with a look of disbelief on his face. "Do you really think Cassie was involved?"

"I have no idea, but we'll certainly be in a better position to make an educated guess after tomorrow, not that I know where we'll go with it. I'll talk to Roger later on and see what he has to say. His background is in criminal law, so I'm sure he'll have some thoughts on it."

"You mentioned Stanley had given you a gun. I agree with him that you could be in danger. I really do need to get this dinner going, but I'd like to talk to you at length tomorrow, say after breakfast?"

"Yes, and I'd like to pick your brain some more. I'm kind of at a loss as what to do at this point."

"I don't blame you. Maybe a few hours away from it will give you some insights."

As she left the kitchen she heard the ATVs pulling into the circular driveway of the lodge, signaling that the guests had returned from the afternoon hunt. Sam hurried to find Jack, so he could be served his evening meal. Liz saw Roger entering the lodge, and she joined him. "Well, Mr. Hunter, how was your afternoon?" she asked as they walked up the stairs.

"It was fabulous. I've got the hang of it now, and I really did well. The man I hunted with this afternoon, that dentist you talked to last night at dinner, and the guide both really complimented me. I'll probably never do this again, but it's been the experience of a lifetime. I always wondered what it would be like to hunt at a premier lodge, and now I know. Plus, I'm not even addressing the fabulous food we've had. To change the subject, what did you do this afternoon?" he asked as he pulled his key out of his pocket, put it in the lock, and opened the door to their suite.

"I'll tell you all about it after dinner when we get back to the room. It's a long story, and I don't want to be late for dinner. We only have tonight and tomorrow, and as good as Wes' food is, I don't want to miss it."

"So it's Wes now?" Roger said, raising an eyebrow.

"Yes, and as I said, I'll tell you all about it after dinner. It was quite the day, and you can lower your eyebrow," she said laughing.

"Sweetheart, where you're concerned, that doesn't surprise me in the least, but I definitely want to hear all about it."

They changed clothes and walked down the stairs to the sound of convivial voices telling war stories about the day's hunt. Sam was waiting for Liz and accompanied Roger and her into the great room. She smiled at several people and once again silently complimented Jack for not decorating the walls with stuffed animals. His taste, or whoever had done the interior design, resulted in a look best described as chic hunt club elegance.

They went into the dining room and found their name cards along with the evening's menu. Liz looked at it and saw where the main entrée was going to be a skillet roasted chicken breast with mushroom gravy, along with creamy risotto studded with pancetta, and garlic brussel sprouts. Her mouth watered just reading about what was to come.

Her dining companions were delightful. The man on her left, Rich Jessup, was a cosmetic surgeon from New York who had wanted to come to The Big T Lodge for years, but only recently had found the time to get away from his busy medical practice. On her right was David Noyes, the owner of an insurance company which specialized in insuring private aircraft. He was from Miami and had flown to the lodge in his private jet. David said if he was going to be the president of a company which insured private planes, he might as well assure his customers that he thought private planes were not only an easier way to travel than flying commercially, but that they were safer. He told her most airplane crashes weren't the fault of the plane, but the fault of the pilot.

When dinner ended Roger looked across the table and with his finger, pointed upward, indicating he wanted to go up to their room. Liz told Rich and David how much she'd enjoyed talking with them and walked up the stairs with Roger and Sam who had joined them as they left the dining room. As soon as they walked into their room, Sam laid down on the colorful braided rug and promptly fell asleep.

"Liz, I don't know if your dinner was as good as mine, but please ask Wes, as you now call him, if you can have the recipe for the risotto. That was fabulous, and the pancetta in it was a nice touch. I've never had anything quite like that."

"Nor have I, and yes, I will ask Wes for the recipe. We're best buds now, so I imagine he'll give it to me."

"Best buds? With the chef? Why am I not surprised?" he asked.

"Roger, it's been quite a day. Why don't you sit down? I've got a lot to tell you." She began with the email she'd received from Sean late that morning.

CHAPTER THIRTY

Jesse and the other server, Zach, carried the dishes from the dining room into the kitchen and began the chore of cleaning up after the evening meal. A few moments later there was a knock on the kitchen door.

"I'll get it," Cassie said to Wes who was in the pantry sitting at his desk working on the menu for the following day.

She opened the door and saw Emilio DeLuise standing there. "Cassie, would you do me a favor? I have to make some calls to Italy, the difference in time changes you know, and I'd really like to sip on a brandy while I'm making them. I want to take a shower first, so would you please bring a brandy up to me in about half an hour?"

"Of course. I'd be happy to, Mr. DeLuise."

Thirty minutes later she walked into the pantry, and told Wes she was taking a brandy up to Emilio DeLuise's room, and she'd be back shortly. He nodded, not paying much attention, completely absorbed in what he was doing.

Cassie carried the brandy up the stairs and knocked on Emilio's door. He quickly opened it, took it from her, and thanked her for bringing it. She turned to walk back downstairs when she thought she heard a woman in room ten say the word "Paul." She assumed it was

Liz Langley as the names Roger and Liz Langley were posted next to the door of their room. She bent down next to their door to give the appearance she was looking for something on the floor in case someone happened to question why she was there. She listened intently to the voice coming from inside the room.

"Roger," Liz said, "the sheriff agreed to exhume the bodies of Paul Sowers and a woman named Julia. I don't remember her last name. Anyway, the sheriff and a medical examiner from El Paso are going to Riley in the morning to conduct an examination of their exhumed bodies. The sheriff decided to take this action based on the test results that Sean obtained from the bottle of liquid I sent him. I told you the analysis determined potassium cyanide had been added to the liquid in the bottle that was next to Milt's body. That, along with the mortuary owner's strong feeling that Paul and Julia might have been poisoned several years ago, was enough for the sheriff to order that the bodies be exhumed and tested for the presence of toxic chemical substances.

"It won't tell us who murdered Milt, but if it's determined that Paul and Julia were also poisoned, sure makes me think Cassie might have been involved. Plus, there was the photo of the poster I showed you of Milt with the bullseye painted over his heart. Is it a confession? No, but it sure seems to me like some law enforcement officials might think there's enough circumstantial evidence to start an investigation. So, Roger, what do you think?"

Cassie didn't stay around to hear what Roger thought. Her heart was pounding wildly as she stood up and raced down the stairs, her mind frantically searching for something she could do before she was implicated or worse yet, arrested for murder. She walked into the kitchen as Jessie and Zack were finishing up. "Thanks, guys. Looks like you're done. Have a good rest of the night. See you in the morning."

She walked into the pantry where Wes had just finished with his menu preparations for the following day. She glanced at him and said, "Chef, why don't I come in a little early tomorrow morning and make those chocolate chip bran muffins everyone loves? You've been working so hard lately it will give you a little extra time off in the morning."

"That's very thoughtful of you, Cassie. I really appreciate it. I don't think I've had a day off in weeks and even a couple of extra hours will probably be enough to re-energize me. I think that's pretty much everything for tonight. You know where all the ingredients are for the muffins. See you in the morning," he said, walking out the door and heading for his cabin.

Cassie opened the laptop where the recipes were stored and pulled up the one for bran muffins. *This is the perfect solution to the problem*, she thought. She turned out the lights and walked to her car, convinced her plan would work.

CHAPTER THIRTY-ONE

"Happy hunting," Liz said to Roger the next morning as he prepared for the early duck hunt. "I'll meet you downstairs for breakfast when you get back."

"What's on your agenda today?" he asked.

"Not much. I'll probably finish that book I started yesterday. Matter of fact, think I'll curl up here in bed for a few hours and do just that. Love you." She turned on the light above her side of the bed as Roger opened the door and left, ready for his last day of hunting.

Two hours later Liz decided to get dressed and get a cup of coffee from downstairs. She remembered Jack telling the guests on the first night they arrived that a big pot of coffee was always available in the kitchen after the guests left for the duck hunt. She walked down the stairs and went to the kitchen, Sam by her side. She knocked on the door, and it was quickly opened by Cassie. Sam let out a low deep throated growl.

"Sam, no. Stop that. Good morning, Cassie. What do I smell? It's heavenly."

"Oh, I'm baking some chocolate chip bran muffins. They'll be ready in about fifteen minutes. I'll bring one up to your room when they're finished."

"I can't ask you to do that. I'm sure you have a number of other things you need to do to get ready for breakfast," Liz said as she poured herself a cup of coffee.

"I insist," Cassie said. "It's not a problem at all. One of the things we try to do here at the lodge is give special service to our guests. I'll see you in a little while."

Liz carefully balanced her coffee cup so she wouldn't spill any of its contents on the carpeting on the stairs, which had been custom-made for the lodge and reflected the greens, reds, browns, and greys that were predominant throughout the lodge. She and Sam walked back to her suite, and she sat on the bed, legs outstretched, reading her book and enjoying her coffee. Sam was on the braided rug, his self-appointed bed, and was soon asleep.

Fifteen minutes later there was a knock on the door. Sam raised his head and growled. Liz shushed him and opened the door to a smiling Cassie. "I'll put it on the table over there," Cassie said, walking into the room. The door swung shut behind her, but without a firm hand closing it, it didn't close completely.

"Please sit down, Mrs. Langley. I'd like you to enjoy your bran muffin, because it's the last thing you'll ever eat," Cassie said as she turned around, a gun in her hand.

"What are you talking about?" Liz asked in astonishment, her eyes wide with fright at the sight of the gun in Cassie's hand.

A demonic look came over Cassie's face and she said, "Eat that muffin, or I'll kill you like I did the other three. You're going to die a nice death from an overdose of sleeping pills, but first you're going to write a suicide note to your husband telling him you're sorry to ruin his trip. You're going to write that you couldn't go on any longer, knowing you were living a lie. You're going to tell him you've been hearing a mysterious voice in your head and seeing things that you don't think are really there. In other words, he shouldn't believe anything you've said lately. Here's the pen and paper. Now start writing, or I'll shoot you. I'll dictate the words. Begin with Dear Roger."

Neither one of them noticed that Sam had left the room.

*****

When Wes walked into the kitchen he smiled as he deeply inhaled the aroma of the freshly baked muffins. He walked over to his desk and looked at the menu he'd written down the evening before. He looked through the papers again, searching for the one that listed the side dishes he was planning on serving along with the prime rib that was the main course for tonight's dinner. He couldn't find it anywhere

Darn. I put a bunch of stuff in the trash just before I left last night. Maybe I accidentally threw it in there. He walked over to the trash barrel and started pawing through it, looking for the missing piece of paper. He noticed a pill bottle and thought it was strange that a pill bottle would be in the trash barrel. He and Cassie were the only ones who used this particular trash barrel. When Jesse and Zach were hired they'd been instructed to take all of their trash out to the big barrel next to the back door of the kitchen, so the one inside wouldn't fill up quite so quickly. He read the label on the bottle and felt his blood run cold. Everything came together for him in a single crashing moment, and at the same time he heard Sam growling at the kitchen door. He opened the door and said, "Sam, come! I need you to take me to Liz and Cassie." The big dog stood there quivering.

Of course Cassie wanted to make bran muffins this morning, he thought as he reached into the cabinet for the activated charcoal he kept on hand in case a guest inadvertently ate or drank something poisonous. *The pill bottle was for sleeping pills. I'll bet Cassie found out Liz discovered that Milt had been murdered and decided to do away with her. I just hope I'm not too late.*

"Sam, take me to Liz!" he said firmly to the big dog as he grabbed a gun from his desk drawer and stuck it in his pocket. Sam got behind him and nudged him, indicating he was to go upstairs. Wes bounded up the steps two at a time. As they got close to the Langley's suite Sam began to growl again. Wes held his hand up, indicating for Sam to be quiet. He noiselessly peeked through the slightly opened door and saw Cassie with a gun in her hand standing over Liz, who looked like she was asleep.

"Drop your gun, Cassie, or I'll shoot," Wes shouted. Cassie instantly whirled around and fired a wild shot that missed Wes and crashed into the door jamb. Wes's shot at Cassie was more accurate, hitting her hand, and causing her gun to drop to the floor. He quickly picked it up.

"Sam, come! Cassie get down on the floor on your stomach and put your hands out in front of you. Sam, stand guard on Cassie." The big dog put his two front paws on Cassie's back, effectively keeping her from moving. Wes was a big man and although Liz was tall, he outweighed her by almost one hundred pounds. He easily slung her over his shoulder and took her into the bathroom. He shoved some activated charcoal down her throat and forced water down it as well, at the same time praying.

A few minutes later Liz began to gag and as she came to, he forced her head over the toilet. Within moments she shook her head and he heard her say, "Enough. I'm okay."

"Thank heavens. Stay where you are for a few more minutes. I need to make sure Sam has a handle on Cassie."

He looked out the door of the bathroom and saw that Sam was taking his job very seriously. There was no way Cassie could move with the big dog on top of her.

"Wes, I'm all right. How did you know to come up to my room?"

"I'll tell you all about it later. Didn't you tell me the sheriff was going to oversee the job of having the bodies of Paul and Julia dug up this morning and then tested by the forensic medical examiner? Is he at the mortuary?"

"Yes, that's what I was told by Stanley."

"Good. I'll call and tell him what's happened. He can come out here and arrest Cassie for attempted murder, and my guess would be for the murder of three more people, namely Milt, Paul, and Julia. Do you have the number of the mortuary?"

"Yes. My cell phone's on the desk. It's in the contacts list. Actually, I feel pretty shaky. I don't think I can stand up. Could you bring it to me?"

"Stay where you are. I'll get it and call him. I want to keep my gun on Cassie."

Wes made the call and in less than an hour the sheriff, one of his deputies, and Stanley Gordon raced up the stairs and into Liz's room. Wes had helped Liz into bed, and she was resting. While the sheriff and his deputy quickly handcuffed Cassie, led her down the stairs, and put her in the sheriff's patrol car, Stanley said, "I want to hear exactly what happened, but I'll wait until the sheriff returns, so you don't have to tell your story twice. I guess you didn't have a chance to use the gun I gave you."

"No, I got blindsided, but it's a good feeling to know I won't have to use it. Thanks again. It's in my purse. Why don't you take it with you?"

"I will, since it looks like you won't need it now."

When the sheriff and his deputy had secured Cassie in the back seat of their patrol car and locked the door, the sheriff returned, leaving his deputy to guard Cassie. He asked Liz and Wes what had happened.

"I went downstairs to get a cup of coffee and smelled something wonderful," Liz said. "Cassie told me that fresh baked chocolate chip bran muffins would be ready in about fifteen minutes, and she'd bring me one. I didn't want to trouble her, but she insisted. When I let her in my room she walked over to the table and put the muffin on it. I didn't see her take a gun from her pocket, but she must have, because when she turned around she pointed it at me.

"Cassie told me she'd shoot me, if I didn't write a suicide note to Roger indicating I was more or less mentally unstable, which she dictated. I had no choice. She gave me the muffin, told me to eat it, and then I'd be asleep for a long time. Again, I had no choice, so I ate it. The next thing I remember is looking at the toilet bowl with Wes holding on to me."

Wes interrupted and said, "So that's how she got you to take the poison. Sheriff, I found an empty sleeping pill bottle in the trash when I was looking for a piece of paper I'd misplaced. Evidently Cassie put the sleeping pills in the muffin mix. I'll be back in a minute," he said as he walked over to the door. "I have no idea if the rest of the muffins had sleeping pills added to them, but I better throw them out. Don't think Jack would be very happy if all of the guests went to sleep permanently after they'd eaten breakfast."

"Liz, how are you feeling now?" Stanley asked.

"Pretty shaky. I think I'll stay here for a little while. I know my husband and the rest of the hunters will be returning soon for breakfast, but I really don't feel up to going down and meeting them."

Wes hurried back into the room. "Liz, I heard that. When Roger gets back I'll have Jesse assure him you're all right and have him come right up to your room. Sheriff, I really need to get down to the kitchen, so I can get breakfast ready. I'm short-handed with Cassie gone. I'll probably have Jesse help me cook and have one of the guides take Jesse's place as a server. If you need anything else from me, I'll be here the rest of the day." He hurried out of the room.

"Liz, I'm going to take these muffin crumbs as evidence," the sheriff said. "They could be crucial to Cassie's case. As we speak, the bodies of Paul and Julia are being tested for any traces of toxic chemical substances. If it turns out they were poisoned, and from what I've seen today, I think there's a very good chance they were, the advice I'd give to Mrs. Sowers is to get a very good attorney, because she's going to need one."

When the sheriff and his deputy had taken Cassie down to the sheriff's car, Sam had laid down on the floor beside Liz's bed, a barrier to anyone who wanted to get near her. Stanley and the sheriff said their goodbyes over the big dog, and Liz assured them she'd rest, and that she was sure she'd feel better in a little while.

"Mrs. Langley, one more thing," the sheriff said. "We all owe you a big thanks for being persistent, first in determining that Milt Huston was poisoned, and secondly for persuading Stanley that the deaths of Paul and Julia needed to be revisited. As sheriff, I have the authority to open those two cases up and also to make the determination that Milt was murdered. I'm going to call his widow and tell her we're certain we've arrested the person who murdered him, and I'm also going to tell her your role in all of this. Is that all right with you?"

"Yes, although I've never met her, I strongly believe she deserves to have some closure concerning the cause of her husband's death. I can't imagine anything worse than wondering if your husband was murdered before you could even tell him you were pregnant. That poor woman!"

"I'll let you know the test results as soon as the medical examiner finishes his work. Now you need to rest. You deserve it and again, thanks!"

For the next half hour Liz was deep in thought, thinking about everything that had happened during the last few days. It seemed better suited to a movie script rather than a famous hunting lodge in west Texas.

Liz felt her strength slowly begin to return, and she decided to email Sean and tell him what had happened. She began, "Sean, you're never going to believe what you're about to read…"

CHAPTER THIRTY-TWO

Liz had just put her laptop back on the table after writing a long email to Sean when Roger flung the door open. "Liz, what's going on? Jesse told me you were up here and wanted to see me. That is so unlike you. Are you all right? You look awfully pale. Liz, you're shaking. What's happened?"

"Better sit down, Roger. It's kind of a long story," she said as the tears she'd been holding back started to flow.

"Liz, Liz, what is it? You never cry. Please, tell me what's going on."

"Roger," she said sniffling, "I just realized how much I love you, and how lucky I am to be alive."

"Well, believe me, I'm pretty glad you are too, but…"

She interrupted him. "It all started after you left this morning." She told him everything concluding with the long email she'd just finished writing to Sean.

"Oh, sweetheart. I can't believe how lucky we are that Wes found that pill bottle. I don't even want to think about what might have happened if he hadn't. Liz, Jack has to be told about this. After all, one murder happened on his property and another one almost did.

I'm going downstairs and getting him. I'd like him to hear it from you."

A few minutes later Jack and Roger entered the room, both of them wearing grim looks. "Liz, Roger tells me Cassie tried to poison you. Please, tell me everything. The reputation of my lodge is at stake here."

Roger looked at him incredulously and said in an angry voice, "The reputation of your lodge? How about my wife almost being murdered by your employee? Think her life is a heck of a lot more important than the reputation of your lodge. Let me tell you something, Jack, with that kind of an attitude I'm inclined to file a lawsuit against you on Liz's behalf seeking damages for the emotional fright and distress you've caused her to suffer. Go ahead, Liz, tell him what happened."

Liz recounted everything that had happened and concluded by saying, "If it hadn't been for Chet Jackson, I wouldn't be talking to you now."

All three of them were quiet for a long time, and then Jack began to speak. He looked down at his hands as he spoke, unwilling to meet Liz's glaze. "Liz, I'm sorry for everything you've been through, and I'm truly glad you're alive. I know I sounded callous a few moments ago, and I apologize for that, but this lodge is my life. My wife died many years ago from cervical cancer, and I didn't know what to do with myself. We never had children, and I was almost suicidal with grief. I'd inherited this property from my parents, and my doctor in El Paso suggested I build a hunting lodge on it. With my elevated blood pressure and stress test failures he felt if I didn't take my own life, I was probably going to die anyway.

"My daddy taught me how to hunt as soon as I was big enough to hold a gun. It's second nature to me. Dogs and guns were my second love, but Abby, my wife, was my first. I built this lodge from the ground up, and I've seen it become perhaps the most prestigious hunting lodge in the Unites States. I'm very proud of what I've done, and I really feel it saved my life.

"I know this is a lot to ask, but would you be willing to say nothing about what's happened to you to the other guests? They'll be leaving tomorrow, so it would just be for the rest of today, and they'll all be out hunting anyway. I'll get in touch with Stanley and the sheriff tomorrow and do whatever they want. Please, give me today. I know what's happened will get out eventually, but perhaps the current guests won't find out about it until much later. If it hits the hunting magazines and media, it could mean the end of my lodge, and I think it would be the end of me. I'm sure my competitors would have a field day with it."

"All right Jack, given those circumstances I'm willing to do as you ask. Now you both better go and get some breakfast. I don't want you to miss the quail hunt."

"Are you crazy, Liz?" Roger asked. "I'm not leaving you alone. I'll stay here with you."

"Fraid not, love. My mind is made up. This is your last chance to hunt, and I want you to have a good time. As a matter of fact, I've decided to go down to the kitchen and see what I can do to help my friend Wes, now that Cassie isn't here to help him. It's the least I can do to repay him for saving my life. Please believe me when I tell you that I really do feel almost back to normal."

"Roger," Jack said, "I think Liz means it. Come on, you paid for this hunt and from what I hear, you really did well yesterday. Might as well go out with a bang, literally. I'm going down to the kitchen and see if I can scare up a couple of breakfasts to take with us, but I promise you, no muffins." He walked over to the door and motioned for Sam to follow him. It had been a rough morning for Sam, and he was perfectly willing to follow his master. Who knew? Maybe his master would feel he deserved a special treat.

"Liz, I'm only going to go if you'll promise me that if you don't feel good at any time, you'll tell Chef Jackson. I'm sure there's someone else he can call on. I'm certain he must have some kind of a back-up plan in place in case either he or Cassie became ill."

"I promise. Now go and have a wonderful last hunt. Actually, I'm looking forward to being Wes' sous chef. Bet I'll learn a lot, and Roger, I'm so glad to be here. I love you so much."

"Likewise, sweetheart, likewise."

CHAPTER THIRTY-THREE

Liz knocked on the kitchen door and heard Wes say, "Come in."

"Hi, Wes," she said. "Thought you could use a couple of extra hands in the kitchen. I'm here to help. Point me in the right direction, and I'll get started."

"Are you kidding me? After what you went through this morning you need more than a couple of hours to recuperate."

"Honest, Wes, I feel great. Believe me, I'm just happy to be alive, considering the alternative. I can never thank you enough for what you did. I shudder to think what might have happened if you hadn't lost that scrap of paper and decided to look in the trash for it. By the way, I've been wondering why you had the activated charcoal here in the kitchen. That's kind of a strange thing to keep on hand."

"If you really feel you're up to it, yes, I could use your help. As far as the charcoal, when I was a sous chef in San Francisco the chef told me once that he felt the most important item in his kitchen was the activated charcoal. He said you could substitute ingredients for everything else, but if someone was inadvertently poisoned, and it happens from time to time, there is no substitute for activated charcoal.

"I've heard of cases where a waiter or waitress was tired and not really paying attention to what they were doing. Instead of filling a glass with sparking water they poured lye or whatever in it and took it to a customer. Anyway, the chef told me to always have some handy for that one in a million time when you're going to need it.

"When I saw the sleeping pill bottle and the muffins, I don't know how I knew, but I did, that Cassie was going to poison you. I didn't even think. I just grabbed the bottle with the charcoal and my gun, both of which came in handy. Actually, it's the first time I've ever had to use either one. I keep the gun in the desk because I often spend a lot of time completely alone here, and the lodge is pretty remote. Jack insisted on it, and a couple of the guides taught me to shoot. Anyway, glad to be of help. Now, let's get started, but first I want you to promise me something."

"Of course. What?"

"You might have a delayed reaction to everything that happened this morning or even because of the events of the last few days. It for any reason you don't feel quite right, let me know immediately. If you can promise me that, I'll let you help me."

"That I can. What's first?"

"Here's the menu," Wes said. "We're serving prime rib, scalloped cheesy potatoes, green beans with slivered almonds, and for dessert, lemon buttermilk pie with blueberries steeped in Grand Marnier and topped with grated white chocolate."

"I think I've died and gone to heaven. That sounds absolutely decadent."

"It is, but we want the guests to leave with a good taste, literally. I made sweet rolls for them to take when they leave for the airport or whatever tomorrow morning. Some of them have very early flights out of El Paso, and a few who have their own planes like to get an early start. You can start by wrapping each sweet roll in plastic wrap, then put two of the sweet rolls and a napkin in each paper bag. When you're finished put them on the long table in the pantry, and I'll put them out in the dining room after dinner."

Liz carefully wrapped the yeasty rolls in plastic wrap and placed them in the paper bags as directed. Chef Jackson had filled them with a variety of wonderfully smelling things such as caramel, lemon cream, and berries. Liz knew they'd all be eaten long before any planes took off.

She walked back into the kitchen after taking the last of them to the pantry and said, "What's next?"

Wes wiped his hands on his apron and said, "Are you sure you're up for this? Tell me how you're really feeling."

"I feel absolutely great, but I just need my marching orders."

"In that case I'd like you to prep the green beans by snapping the ends off, breaking them into bite-size pieces and putting them in a big bowl of cold water, so they'll be ready to go. You can also get the slivered almonds from the pantry, lightly toast them in a frying pan, and have them ready for me to add to the green beans when I flash-fry them in a little olive oil."

"No problem. I can do that."

Liz usually cooked for around twelve to fourteen people when she did the evening meals at the Red Cedar Lodge and Spa. She'd prepared green beans many times for her guests, but she decided that preparing for the additional six people made for a lot more work. She easily found the slivered almonds, toasted them, and put them in a bowl next to the stove.

"Here's the recipe for the potatoes. I want it quadrupled," Wes said. And so the afternoon went. Liz became completely absorbed in what she was doing, and when she heard sounds coming from the entryway, she glanced at her watch and realized it must be the hunters returning from the afternoon quail hunt.

"Liz, I'm going to take this platter of different kinds of cheese and crackers out to the great room. I opened the wines a little while ago to let them breathe, and Jesse will tend the bar. You've been a huge help, and I can't thank you enough. Now go on up to your room and get ready to join the other guests in the dining room when dinner is served."

"I've already decided I'll enjoy my dinner here in the kitchen with you, Wes. I'm not going to abandon you now. You've got hungry guests out there, and I know there's more to do in here, although I'm having trouble concentrating on anything other than the smell of those three gorgeous prime rib roasts in the oven."

"Well, don't say I didn't offer, but if you're serious I'd love to have you help me. We make a good team."

"Give me a couple of minutes to go upstairs and tell Roger, although I know he'll agree it's the right thing to do."

She was back in a few minutes and gave Wes the thumbs up sign when she walked into the kitchen. The next two hours were a blur for Liz as she plated, garnished, and did whatever needed to be done to get the final meal for the guests on the table with a flair for presentation. She doubted that the guests ever suspected she was filling in for Cassie, and she was sure they didn't know that Cassie was in the county jail, charged with murder.

CHAPTER THIRTY-FOUR

Just after Jesse and Zach had cleared the last dessert plates, there was a knock on the kitchen door. Liz was standing nearby and opened it. "Hi sweetheart," Roger said, "I just wanted to check and see how you're feeling."

"Roger, I've never had so much fun in my life. I've really learned a lot. I feel like I've been at an exclusive cooking school. Wes has given me a gazillion cooking tips. I just hope I can remember them all."

"Thanks for allowing Liz to help me in the kitchen. I know said I could do it by myself, but truthfully, I'm not sure I could have."

"Wes, I'm glad she could help you, but believe me, I don't allow Liz to do anything. The lady does whatever she wants," he said, fondly smiling at her.

"Roger, why don't you go on up to the room," Liz said. "As I recall, our flight leaves El Paso around nine in the morning, and it's a bit of a drive there, so we probably better pack tonight. I'll be up in a little while. I want to help Wes put the food away and finish up. Plus, I haven't had time to eat dinner, and there is no way I'm leaving here without having some of that prime rib and the dessert that's definitely been calling my name."

"Take your time. I've got to get my hunting gear organized and packed in its special bag. That's going to take a little time."

When the last of the food had been put away, Wes and Liz sat down to dinner and poured themselves a glass of wine. "Liz, in many ways this is my favorite time of the day. Everything's been done, it's all gone well, and I can relax until tomorrow, and then I do it all over again. I really want to thank you for not only helping me tonight, but also causing me to make a decision that's probably long overdue."

Liz put her fork down and looked at him. "I have no idea what you're talking about."

"I think I mentioned to you that if I found out that Milt was murdered, I might rethink whether or not I wanted to stay here at the hunting lodge. I understand Jack's reasoning for not telling the guests about Milt's murder or about Cassie, but I don't want to work for someone who thinks like that. It's time for me to open up my own restaurant. I'm going back to the town where I grew up and open one. I go back there from time to time to visit my parents, and I've noticed that the town has been able to support a couple of good restaurants. I'm going to see what happens when I open mine, but I'm optimistic it will work out okay."

"Wes, if the food I've eaten here in the last few days is any indication of what you're capable of cooking, the town won't only support it, I predict you will definitely be the recipient of a Michelin star. Just think, I can say I knew you when," she said laughing.

They both heard the sound of a ringing phone. Liz walked over to where she'd put her purse earlier in the afternoon, took her phone out of it, and answered the call. She didn't recognize the number. "This is Liz Langley."

"Mrs. Langley, it's Sheriff Brown. I called you earlier, but I guess you didn't get my message asking you to call me."

"I'm sorry, Sheriff. I decided to help Chef Jackson in the kitchen, and I've been focused on that for the last few hours. We're just finishing up."

"Well, Mrs. Langley, I called to tell you your instincts were right about everything. The medical examiner confirmed that both Paul and Julia were poisoned. Both of them had ingested large amounts of sleeping pills and potassium cyanide."

"I'm sure Stanley feels vindicated," Liz said, "because he had a feeling for all these years that something wasn't quite right about their deaths."

"Yes," Sheriff Brown said. "I talked to him earlier this evening, and he said if it hadn't been for what you discovered about Mr. Huston's death he never would have pursued it. I hate to look at it this way, but maybe that's the justification for his death, although I don't think murder is ever justified."

"What will happen to Cassie now?" Liz asked.

"Kind of an interesting thing happened. I guess she's pretty religious, and when I told her she could make one phone call, I figured it would be to an attorney, leastways that's always been my experience in the past when suspects get to make their allotted phone call. But she called her pastor, a man by the name of Billy Bob Benson. I've never met the man, but I've heard he's a real fire and brimstone old-time preacher, but here's the kicker."

"I'm all ears," Liz said.

"Billy Bob told her if she was the one who killed Paul and Julia, and if she didn't admit it, she'd never be admitted into heaven. He told her the only way she could get there was to cleanse her soul and admit what she'd done. She was quiet for a long time, and then she told me she'd murdered both of them as well as Milt Huston, and she hoped the court would be lenient on her when she was sentenced. I told her I couldn't promise her anything, but when a public defender was appointed for her, he might be able to work out some kind of a deal. Don't that beat all?"

"So it really is over. All the deaths have been accounted for, and she was the one responsible. Thank you for calling to tell me."

"Mrs. Langley, the citizens of the county are very much indebted to you, and I for one want to thank you again."

"Sheriff, I had no idea this would be the outcome when I sent that bottle of red beet juice to San Francisco. I'm as surprised as anyone. Strange, isn't it, the secrets that are sometimes buried for years and then are suddenly uncovered."

"Yes, ma'am, except in this case, the secrets have been made public. You have yourself a good rest of the night. You sound pretty good. Feelin' all right?"

"Yes, thanks, I feel absolutely great. Good night."

She looked over at Wes. "You heard?"

"Yes. I can't believe all this time I was working with a murderer. When I hire the staff for my restaurant, I'm going to be far more careful than I was with her."

"Wes, from what I've seen of this area I'm not sure you had much of a choice. If you don't mind, I'm going to do an Emilio, but instead of taking a brandy to my room, I'm going to take a piece of that pie. I don't know if I'll see you in the morning, but if not, I wish you all the luck in the world, and I've really enjoyed being with you the last few days. Here's my business card with my email address on it. I'd like to stay in touch."

"After finding the sister I never thought I'd have, there is no way you're going to get rid of me that easily," he said lightly kissing her on the cheek. "Off to your husband and a good's night sleep. You've put in a full day. I'll be in touch."

CHAPTER THIRTY-FIVE

The day after they returned to Red Cedar, Roger walked into the lodge kitchen with a copy of the San Francisco Chronicle in his hand. "Liz, there's an article in here about Milt Huston. Thought you'd want to see it."

"Roger, please summarize it for me. I'm trying to make that pecan pie you liked so much, and I can't stop to read it."

"It says Milt Huston died on a hunting trip when he was in Texas. His widow decided to hold a closed family service for him. Evidently there will be a special election to fill his Attorney General position. It made no mention of him being murdered. I guess his widow didn't want the media frenzy that would have come with that revelation."

"If I was a betting person, I'd bet she's trying to save every ounce of her strength in order to deal with her pregnancy. My heart goes out to her," Liz said.

"So does mine, but at least you were able to ease any fears she might have eventually had about there possibly being a killer on the loose. I'm sure it crossed her mind whether or not she could have been a target as well."

"Roger, I'm so glad it's over now. We're back home, the guest cottages are completely sold out, and quite frankly, I'm glad there wasn't much press about Milt's death or those of Paul and Julia. I'd just as soon people didn't know I had anything to do with solving more murders. At some point it could adversely affect my business here at the lodge and spa. I mean who wants to stay where the owner is constantly getting involved in solving murder cases? If I were a guest, I might begin to wonder if I was next on the list."

"Liz, as long as you keep serving the food you do, and if you could master that pie, I think you could solve hundreds more murders, and people would still come here, just for the food."

"Out, out! If you want me to get this pie crust right, leave me to my pastry," she said laughing. "You do realize that if it wasn't because I love you so much, there is no way in the world I would even try to master this impossible task."

"Liz, everything is possible. The impossible just takes longer. I read that in one of Dan Brown's books, you know the guy that wrote The Da Vinci Code. I think you and your pie crust are one of those things."

He preferred to ignore the piece of dough she threw at his back as he walked out of the kitchen wearing a grin on his face.

RECIPES

RISOTTO WITH PANCETTA AND MUSHROOMS

Ingredients

8 thin slices of pancetta (I prefer this, but if you can't find it, you can substitute bacon)

1 tbsp. olive oil

1 pound mixed mushrooms, thickly sliced (This completely depends on what you can find at the market. Sometimes my only choices are the brown and white ones. Once you start buying the others, it can get a little pricey. Be forewarned)

¼ tsp. sea salt

3 tbsp. unsalted butter (I always use unsalted, so I can control the amount of salt in the dish. If you use salted butter, you're at the mercy of the butter producer)

1 tsp. finely chopped fresh parsley or tarragon

5 cups chicken stock (If you're worried about too much salt being in non-homemade stock, use low-sodium stock)

1 garlic clove, smashed (I use the blade of a heavy knife. Whack it, remove the papery peel, then smash it again)

1 shallot, minced

1 ½ cups Arborio rice (Don't think you can substitute this type of rice with another variety. Believe me, if you use a different type, the dish will not turn out well!)

½ cup freshly grated Parmesan cheese plus ¼ cup shavings for garnish
2 tbsp. heavy cream
Fresh ground pepper

Directions

Preheat the oven to 250 degrees or if you have a plate warmer setting, use that. Place four shallow soup bowls in it. Cook the pancetta in a frying pan until crisp. Drain on paper towels and crumble.

Heat the oil in a large skillet over high heat. Add the mushrooms, season with ¼ teaspoon sea salt, and cook over high heat, stirring until they begin to sweat. (In other words, start losing their juices.) Transfer the mushrooms and the liquid to a strainer set over a bowl. Lightly press on the mushrooms with the back of a spoon, reserving the liquid. Wipe the skillet clean and add 1 tablespoon of butter. Return the mushrooms to the skillet and cook for about three minutes or until they become brown. Add the parsley, turn the heat to low, cover and keep warm.

In a medium saucepan, combine the chicken stock with the reserved mushroom liquid and bring to a simmer, then reduce the heat to low. In a large deep skillet melt 1 tablespoon of butter. Add the garlic and cook over medium heat for one minute. (You don't want it to brown.) Add the minced shallot and cook until softened. Add the rice and stir until the grains are thoroughly coated with butter.

Slowly add 1 cup of the hot chicken stock to the pan and cook, stirring constantly, until the rice has absorbed most of the stock, approximately 1 to 2 minutes. Cook the risotto, adding the stock 1 cup at a time and stirring constantly between additions until each cup is absorbed. Continue to cook the risotto until it has a creamy consistency, about 20 minutes.

Remove the risotto from the heat and stir in the Parmesan cheese, cream, and remaining tablespoon of butter. Season with salt and pepper to taste and transfer to the warm soup bowls. Garnish with pancetta, and Parmesan shavings. Serve and enjoy!

PECAN PIE WITH VANILLA BEAN ICE CREAM AND BOURBON MOLASSES SAUCE

Pie Crust Ingredients (May be made in advance)

1 ½ cups all-purpose flour
½ tsp. salt
¼ cup unsalted butter plus more for buttering pie plate
4-5 tbsp. ice water

Directions

Coat a deep 9-inch pie plate with butter and set aside. In a large bowl, combine the flour and the salt. Cut in the butter with a pastry blender (well worth the money and a lot less messy than doing it with your hands. If you don't have one you can use your fingers to mix the flour with the butter. Some people use two forks or two knives to work the butter into the flour. Your choice.) Keep at it until the mixture resembles coarse meal. Gradually add ice water and with a wooden spoon, mix until a ball of dough is formed.

Put the dough onto a lightly floured sheet of plastic wrap and form it into a disc. Dust the top of the dough with flour and place another sheet of plastic wrap on top. Use a rolling pin and roll from the center out until the dough is round and about 1/8-inch in thickness. Remove the top piece of the plastic wrap and lay the dough across the pie plate. Remove the remaining piece of plastic wrap. Press the dough lightly into the bottom and sides of the pie plate. Cover the plate with a piece of plastic wrap and place in the freezer for at least 30 minutes or overnight.

CHEF JACKSON'S PECAN PIE

Ingredients

1 ½ cups pecan pieces
3 large eggs
1 cup sugar
¾ light corn syrup
2 tbsp. unsalted melted butter
½ tsp. salt
1 sheet of aluminum foil

Directions

Preheat the oven to 350 degrees. Spread the pecans in a single layer on a baking sheet. Bake them for 8 to 10 minutes or until toasted. Stir together the rest of the ingredients. Remove the pie shell from the freezer and pour the filling in it. Bake for 55 minutes or until set, placing aluminum foil over the pie after 20 minutes to prevent excessive browning. Remove from oven.

BOURBON MOLASSES SAUCE

Ingredients

¾ cup sugar
¼ cup water plus 2 tbsp., divided
3 tbsp. bourbon
3 tbsp. unsalted butter
1 ½ tbsp. molasses
¼ tsp. salt
Pastry brush (or any other type of brush)

Directions

Bring the sugar and 2 tablespoons water to a boil in small heavy saucepan over medium heat, stirring until the sugar dissolves. Using a pastry brush dipped in cold water, wash down any sugar crystals from the side of the pan. Boil, without stirring, swirling the pan occasionally until the color becomes a dark amber. Remove from heat and stir in the bourbon, butter, molasses, and salt. Return to heat and simmer, stirring to dissolve any hardened caramel if necessary (Can be made ahead and reheated.)

Assembly:
Pie crust
Pecan pie
Vanilla bean ice cream (Don't skimp here. Treat yourself to the expensive stuff. You've come this far and believe me, it will be worth it when you taste the finished produce!)
Bourbon molasses sauce
Slice the pie into 8 pieces and plate as many pieces as needed. Using an ice cream scoop, put one scoop of the ice cream on the warm pie. Top with 2 tablespoons of the sauce. Enjoy!

LUMP CRAB MEAT AND CITRUS SALAD WITH CHARDONNAY DRESSING (SERVES 4)

Dressing Ingredients:
2 tbsp. Chardonnay or white vinegar
1 tsp. Dijon mustard
1 tsp sugar
5 tbsp. olive oil

Directions:
Whisk together the chardonnay or vinegar, mustard, and sugar in a small bowl. Slowly add the olive oil to the mixture, whisking until it has all been incorporated. Set aside. (May be made ahead and refrigerated.)

Salad Ingredients:
2 cups lump crabmeat
1 orange, peeled and sectioned
1 grapefruit, peeled and sectioned

16 leaves romaine lettuce
1 tsp. chopped chives for garnish
4 cylindrical glass sundae dishes

Directions:
Gently combine the crabmeat, orange, and grapefruit in a bowl.

Assembly:
Line the sundae dishes with the romaine leaves. Divide the crabmeat, orange, and grapefruit evenly and place in the sundae dishes. Spoon 2 tablespoons of the dressing over each mixture and top each one with ¼ teaspoon chives. Enjoy!

LEMON SOUFFLE PANCAKES WITH BLUEBERRY MAPLE SYRUP

Syrup Ingredients:
2 tbsp. butter
1 cup maple syrup
1 cup fresh blueberries, rinsed

Directions:
Place ingredients in a small sauce pan over medium heat. Stir occasionally until the butter is melted. Turn heat to low and keep warm until ready to serve.

Pancake Ingredients:
2 cups all-purpose flour
2 tbsp. sugar
1 tsp. baking soda
½ tsp. salt
2 large eggs, yolks and whites separated
1 ½ cups buttermilk
2 tsp. grated lemon peel
3 tbsp. lemon juice
Put bowl and beaters in freezer for beating egg whites

Directions:

Turn oven to 250 degrees or use warm if you have that setting. In a large bowl combine the flour, sugar, baking soda, and salt. In a small bowl whisk together the egg yolks, buttermilk, grated lemon, lemon juice, and 2 tablespoons butter. Take the bowl and beaters out of the freezer and whip the egg whites until they hold stiff peaks. Pour the buttermilk mixture into the flour mixture and stir to blend. Gently fold in the egg whites.

Butter a frying pan or griddle over medium heat. Pour batter in ½ cup portions onto the pan or griddle, being careful that the portions don't touch each other. Cook until golden brown on each side, turning once. Keep the finished ones warm in the oven and repeat the process to cook the remaining pancakes.

Serve the pancakes with the warm syrup. Enjoy!

AVOCADOS WITH CHILLED BROCCOLI CHEDDAR CHEESE SOUP

Ingredients:

1 packet of cheddar cheese broccoli soup (I'm not a big fan of canned soup. Far prefer the packets of soup, and they're available pretty much everywhere)
1 ½ cups cheddar cheese, grated
1 cup broccoli florets (I use small prepackaged florets that come in a plastic bag)
2 avocados, cut in half with about 2 tbsp. flesh scooped out (Leave enough in there to form a boat shape)
8 lettuce leaves
Chives, chopped for garnish
Salsa Verde for garnish (There are a lot of bottled brands available. I don't really have a preference)

Directions:

Place 4 salad plates and forks in the refrigerator to chill. Prepare the soup according to directions on packet. Add 1 cup of cheddar cheese and broccoli florets and cook until florets have lost their crispness. If you want a thicker consistency add the additional ½ cup grated cheddar cheese. You can enjoy a bowl of hot soup at this point. Refrigerate the rest.

Assembly:

Place 2 lettuce leaves on a chilled plate. Place one avocado half on each plate and spoon chilled soup into each half. Garnish with chives and/or Salsa Verde. Enjoy!

Amazing Ebooks & Paperbacks for FREE

Go to www.dianneharman.com/freepaperback.html and get your FREE copies of Dianne's books and Dianne's favorite recipes immediately by signing up for her newsletter.

Once you've signed up for her newsletter you're eligible to win autographed paperbacks. One lucky winner is picked every week. Hurry before the offer ends.

ABOUT THE AUTHOR

Dianne lives in Huntington Beach, California, with her husband, Tom, a former California State Senator, and her boxer dog, Kelly. Her passions are cooking, reading, and dogs, so whenever she has a little free time, you can either find her in the kitchen, playing with Kelly in the back yard, or curled up with the latest book she's reading.

Her award winning books include:

Cedar Bay Cozy Mystery Series
Kelly's Koffee Shop, Murder at Jade Cove, White Cloud Retreat, Marriage and Murder, Murder in the Pearl District, Murder in Calico Gold, Murder at the Cooking School, Murder in Cuba, Trouble at the Kennel

Liz Lucas Cozy Mystery Series
Murder in Cottage #6, Murder & Brandy Boy, The Death Card, Murder at The Bed & Breakfast, The Blue Butterfly, Murder at the Big T Lodge

High Desert Cozy Mystery Series
Murder & The Monkey Band, Murder & The Secret Cave, Murdered by Country Music

Midwest Cozy Mystery Series
Murdered by Words

Coyote Series
Blue Coyote Motel, Coyote in Provence, Cornered Coyote

Website: www.dianneharman.com
Blog: www.dianneharman.com/blog
Email: dianne@dianneharman.com

Newsletter
If you would like to be notified of her latest releases please go to www.dianneharman.com and sign up for her newsletter.

Made in the USA
Middletown, DE
23 July 2016